THE SECRET PEOPLE

THE
SECRET
PEOPLE

MADELAINE DUKE

Illustrated by Ken Longtemps

Doubleday & Company, Inc.
Garden City, New York

CONTENTS

*For Andrew
and Antonia Coe*

THE SECRET PEOPLE

Journey to Lake Disappointment

IT'S GOING TO BE ROUGH," I warned young Ellwood. And sure enough my little aircraft started pitching and sliding sideways. "Hold tight." I banked. The sudden rush of air deadened the sound of the engines. As the plane lost height, the sharp rocks below came leaping into the sunlight—out of the dust that always hovered over the mines. "All right?" I turned and took a look at Ellwood.

He didn't answer. His thick, sun-tanned hands were clasped tight over the safety belt and he was staring out into space. I couldn't be sure, but I thought he was scared.

"We're down to three thousand feet," I said. "Low enough for you?"

Peter, beside me, glanced at the control panel. "You promised you'd fly her at two thousand feet."

"Bit rough."

"Safe?" Peter opened up the survey map on his knees.

"Sure it's safe."

"Go down then," snapped Ellwood. "I don't care *what* you do. If you crash this flea of an airplane it's *your* neck too."

Peter laughed. "Don't you worry about our pilot. Mac knows how to handle a Cessna."

"Okay, Peter, you know the guy." Ellwood still sounded unfriendly, but he looked less worried. "I guess I'm used to jets."

"How did you get to Alice Springs last time?" asked Peter.

"On the Ghan train. I went to Alice just the one time . . . when I was a kid."

That must have been all of ten years ago when a small party of Americans had arrived in the center of Australia and set up a technical base. I seemed to remember that it had been a kind of observatory for spotting underground atomic tests on the Asian continent. Ellwood's father must have been a member of that American team ten years ago. Ellwood would have been twelve or thirteen then. That fitted in with what Peter had told me about my young American passenger—about his being a mining engineer who had recently finished his training in the United States, who had then gone to Australia and worked for a mining company at Mount Isa.

And now he had taken a better-paying job and a more exciting one at the other end of Australia. That made sense. But what I couldn't understand was why he had chosen to cross the country the hard way, Peter's way. It wasn't as if he and Peter had been friends. They'd known one another only a few days—since Peter had flown into Mount Isa from Brisbane.

"The American mining engineer's asked for a lift," Peter had told me. "Shall we take him along, Mac?"

I hadn't refused, but I'd warned Peter that fifteen hundred miles was a long way to take a stranger who looked as bad tempered as Ellwood. Besides, the Australian bush is no country for travelers who are accustomed to the armchair comforts of transatlantic jets.

"You're turning back," said Ellwood.

"Not because Mac's in trouble," Peter assured him. "It's just an old custom."

In fact the custom had started eight years ago, on the day when I'd flown Peter to Alice Springs for the first time. He'd stood on the hot airstrip at Mount Isa, a schoolboy fresh from England, and examined my little twin-engined plane as if he knew all about such machines. He'd talked about Rolls engines, speeds and altitudes like these Pommie know-alls who love to hear their own voices but never *listen*. Not for long though. The moment we were airborne, he'd stopped giving me advice on how I should fly my Cessna and used his eyes. We'd flown over Mount Isa and were heading into the bush country when he'd said, "I wish I could see these mine workings again." So I'd banked the

Cessna and turned back, and we'd circled the torn mountains and the men who were digging and blasting out the ore.

I think it was this first sight of the metal-rich rocks that had made Peter think about the stuff of which our earth is made. He had kept on thinking, and his curiosity had led him to the study of rocks. And years later he'd returned to Australia as a qualified geologist.

I am only a pilot of the small planes which serve the Northern Territories of Australia as buses serve the countries of Europe. I know nothing about rocks and whether they contain copper, iron, gold, or some combination of useful metals, but when I fly low over the bush between Mount Isa and Alice Springs, I can well understand why young fellows like Peter and Ellwood get excited about this land.

So, once again, with Peter beside me and Ellwood breathing down my neck, I studied the ground below and got from it the feeling that I was in a place that was as old as the sun that burned down on it.

We saw rocks as red as fire which the heat of the sun and the beat of sandstorms had carved into shapes as alive-looking as people and cattle, lizards and lions. Then came the gray-green patches of mulga grass and clumps of gum trees which appeared from the air as if they were made of silver. Occasionally, among the red of rocks, the gold of the sands, and the silver of those tough trees and grasses, we saw a long bright-green line zigzagging into the distance, way beyond our sight.

"Water," said Peter. "The greenery along this line means there's a watercourse beneath the sands."

"Looks bone dry to me," said Ellwood. "As dry as the Nevada desert."

"The water's there all right," argued Peter. "If this land

were irrigated . . . if the underground springs were properly used . . ."

"Okay, I expect you'd have good grazing for cattle. So why's nothing done about it?"

"It would cost a lot of money."

"So it's useless."

"Not quite."

"Deserts are a lot of nothing. Dead land. I know. We have our deserts in the States."

"In your deserts there are no people."

"No there aren't, aside from folks who travel through on the highways."

"Mac." Peter's forefinger traced a line on his map. "Can you take us about twenty degrees east-southeast?"

"Right." I knew what it was he wanted to find down there among the rocks and the sand.

It was just luck that we found it some ten minutes later— a very small, very faint wisp of smoke.

"Look!" Peter sounded excited. "Look down, Ellwood!"

"A localized sandstorm."

"Wrong. It's a campfire."

"Oh. Just abos, I guess."

"Aboriginals," Peter corrected him coldly. "They're the original inhabitants of this country. . . . Well, there's no reason why *you* should know anything about them."

"Don't tell me. I once lived around here. I saw all I'd ever want to see of the abos. Savages, that's what they are. Good for nothing."

"Without aboriginal stockmen and trackers the white men couldn't run their farms."

"And *with* their abos they have nothing but trouble. What does the black fellow care about the work on a homestead? Does it ever bother *him* that he's needed? When he takes it into his head that he wants to go walkabout, off he goes into the bush, and that's the last his employers see of him for months or even years. Sure, he'll come back . . . when there's something he wants, like tobacco or drink."

"That's not true."

"Aw, Peter. I lived two years in Alice. I had a friend—an abo kid. He was no better than the rest of them."

"Pity you never met *the rest* of them."

Peter was angry, very angry. I could tell from the way he suddenly went silent. He gets so still that you forget he's there. And that's how he stayed until I landed at Alice Springs.

The moment we climbed out of the plane the flies were upon us—the black bushflies that don't bite but tickle and irritate until one can't think of anything but escape, of getting inside a car or a house.

Ellwood, beating off the flies with his hands, made straight for the airport bungalow. But Peter was in no hurry. He walked on to the far end of the landing strip, striding towards an aboriginal boy in blue cotton trousers and a faded shirt. They shook hands like old friends. And there they stayed, on the broiling hot airstrip, the fair-headed Englishman and the young dark fellow, while I sorted out the parcels for the Alice Hospital.

We don't waste any space on our little planes. Alice Springs—a town isolated in the middle of the bush, bang in the center of Australia—depends on all kinds of supplies from the coast.

So, before you take off from Mount Isa, which lies between Brisbane and Alice, you collect packages which can contain anything from women's dresses to medical supplies.

As I lifted down my camping gear, I thought of all the

people who'd told me I was mad to go and spend my holiday in the bush. Three weeks out in nowhere. But I'd
wanted to do it for years. Every time I'd flown over this
country I'd said to myself, "One day I'll be going right
in . . . find out what the bush is like face to face."

I'd been told it's none too friendly, a tough country for
the white man. And we were about to go a long way,
about three hundred miles from Alice to Lake Mackay and
another three hundred from Lake Mackay to Lake Disappointment where the truck was to meet us.

I put my gear together in a separate pile. No, I didn't
mind the prospects of a tough trip. Peter and his family,
the Landsons, could be trusted to have organized the journey
well.

I had just finished the unloading when Anita arrived. Her
station wagon dashed up to Peter and his aboriginal friend
like a dog welcoming its master. It collected the two boys,
went to fetch Ellwood from the bungalow, and swept on. It
stopped within inches of the packages I had stacked on the
runway.

"Good trip, Mac?" Anita jumped down and shook hands
with me.

"Fine, thanks."

Anita is Peter's cousin, but if the two of them were
brother and sister they couldn't look more alike. They are
both tall and lean, with thick, straight, sun-bleached hair,
and gray eyes—the quick eyes of people who pay attention to
the life around them.

Anita had noticed the parcels for the hospital. "We'll
take this lot to the dispensary first," she said. "Then we'll
drive straight on to Ilara. Mother's expecting us for lunch."

"We'll be late," said Peter.

"Never mind. Mother knows. We'll be there by three. You won't be starting before six, will you?"

"Six in the evening?" asked Ellwood.

"That's right. You want to travel when it's cooler. Six o'clock to midnight's the best time. You haven't yet met Tabalu." Anita gently pushed forward Peter's aboriginal friend. "Tabalu will be one of your guides."

Ellwood and the aboriginal, a boy of sixteen or seventeen, eyed one another. On Ellwood's broad face there was an expression of plain mistrust. Tabalu smiled with something like patience and turned away to help Peter with the loading of the station wagon.

"A lot of use *he's* going to be," muttered Ellwood, watching the small black boy trying to lift Peter's gear.

"Yes, a *lot* of use," said Peter, sharply.

Anita laughed. "Tabalu, he special say with all animal." She sounded exactly like an aboriginal, and Tabalu seemed pleased. Even Peter grinned, his anger with Ellwood forgotten. Whatever was meant by *Tabalu, he special say with all animal*, it appeared to be a private joke between the three of them.

"I don't understand, ma'am," said Ellwood.

"You will," Peter promised. "Just wait till you meet the camels."

The camels at Ilara, the homestead of Anita's parents, lay under a clump of ghost gums, looking like heaps of tawny sand. I like animals, and animals usually put up with me, but I've always felt shy of camels. It's the way they look at you—like schoolmasters who have given up hope of ever being able to teach you how to spell or read a map. The camels at Ilara were no exception; they snorted and looked down their curved noses at us. And Ellwood became suspicious.

"Are they coming with us?" he asked.

Peter smiled. "We're going to travel *on* them."

"For crying out loud!" Ellwood sounded worried rather than aggressive.

"On a long journey through the bush, camels are the best transport," said Anita's father. "They don't break down like cars, they don't get stuck in the sand, and they need very little fuel."

"Fuel?" asked Ellwood, foolishly.

"Food and water. A camel can go without a drink for a week or more. And food—do you know a camel's hump is a sort of storage place? This lot," he pointed to the animals resting under the trees, "they've been grazing for several weeks. It means there's enough *fuel* inside them to last until you reach Lake Mackay."

"I didn't know there *were* camels in Australia," admitted Ellwood.

"The early settlers of Central Australia imported them, complete with drivers from Afghanistan. That's why our train to Alice is still called the Ghan. You see, the country was too large and too hot for travel on horseback . . . and in those days there were no cars."

"You still import camels?"

"No. Now they breed in the Northern Territories. They're wild except for those the aboriginals have caught, trained, and domesticated. On our homestead we have no camels. The animals you see here belong to Tabalu's tribe, the Aranda."

"You arranged for the abos to take us *six hundred miles* across this . . . this desert?" Ellwood made no attempt to hide his nervousness.

Mr. Landson put his hand on his shoulder. "It's Coora-cardie, Tabalu's elder brother, who's arranged your trip. He and Peter—occasionally with my daughter Anita—have traveled thousands of miles in the bush. Aboriginals of the Aranda tribe are the safest guides you can have—especially Cooracardie and Tabalu."

Cooracardie joined us for the late lunch in Mrs. Landson's big farm kitchen. He was a man in his early twenties—about the same age as Peter and Anita. Like his kid brother, Tabalu, he was short and slim built, but he looked strong. He somehow reminded me of those bony lads who win Olympic medals for long-distance running. By contrast, Cooracardie's face was a well-covered oval; the nose short, well shaped and on the flat side, the lips full but not as fleshy as certain African Negroes', the eyes large and amber-yellow in color. Cooracardie's hair was cut very short and it was so thick that it had the rich texture of a kangaroo's coat. It was the same dusky black as his skin.

While Mrs. Landson and Anita served us home-grown saddle of beef, baked potatoes, and runner beans, Coora-cardie remained silent. But later, over homemade cakes and coffee, he and Peter talked in a language I had never heard before. Occasionally Anita would listen to their con-versation and add a remark in the same soft, melodious sounds. Mr. Landson explained to us that it was the language of the Aranda tribe.

"My wife and I never managed to pick up more than a few words in Aranda," he said. "But Anita and Peter have made a study of it."

Mrs. Landson laughed. "Anita couldn't help learning Aranda. She was *brought up* by our aboriginal stockmen. It's Peter who took trouble learning aboriginal languages. When he came out to Australia he was already fifteen. Within days of his arrival he met Cooracardie. . . ."

Mr. Landson nodded. "Yes, it was Cooracardie who made him what he is. . . . At heart, Peter's a Centralian; a Central Australian," he explained for Ellwood's benefit.

Ellwood stared at Peter and Cooracardie who were still absorbed in the private conversation which none but Anita could understand. The way Ellwood watched made me realize how little he liked the prospect of traveling hundreds of miles with a couple of black fellows and with a man who looked more at home with the aboriginals than with his own relatives. As for me—I obviously didn't count; not in Ellwood's eyes. I was an old man of thirty who could fly a little airplane, but who didn't know how to get on to a camel's back, let alone how to stay on it for weeks on end.

A camel is not an uncomfortable animal to ride once you've gotten used to the strange dipping and rising motion. Ellwood's animal and mine had been saddled with light cane seats. Peter, Cooracardie, and Tabalu rode without saddle, sitting on rugs.

After the first hour or so, I forgot that I was riding an animal which had spat and snorted at me in a most unfriendly manner. There was too much to see for me to worry about the private feelings of a snooty camel. Above all, there were the changing colors. We were trotting through pale-dun sand which suddenly appeared to catch fire, turning to gold, to orange, and later to deep terra-cotta red. And while I was still gazing at the flaming sands and rocks, they suddenly changed to the strong blue of African violets. Then, as if giant hands had pulled a curtain across the glowing bush, night fell.

It wasn't a dark night though. Far from it. Once my eyes

had become used to the lack of color, I became aware of the shapes of jagged rocks, the pewter gleam of the gum trees. Stars were lighting our way, stars as brilliant as thousands of little white flames. I had never seen them more clearly; the whole sky looked so close to the earth that I had the feeling I could touch it and pluck me a star like picking a flower.

Maybe Ellwood felt the same. Though he was riding beside me, he didn't say a word—not until Peter and the two aboriginal boys halted their camels and Peter said we'd stop and camp for the rest of the night.

While Cooracardie and Tabalu collected gumwood, lit a fire, and put on the teakettle, Ellwood opened up a small bag which I had taken for a camera case. Out came a tape recorder. And within seconds the beautiful night was ruined —for me at any rate. A steel band had started up and some loud-mouthed singer was screaming his head off. Somehow his voice spoiled my sense of being in a faraway place—a place as wonderful and strange as the moon.

Peter came and handed Ellwood and me mugs of tea. "*Must* you play this thing?" he asked.

"Any objection?" Ellwood sounded aggressive.

"No." Peter turned slowly and walked off, away from the campfire, to the clump of gumtrees where the camels and his aboriginal friends were resting.

I'd have liked to be with them, out in the starlit night, away from the pop singer's screams, listening into the silence of the bush. But I couldn't bring myself to leave Ellwood alone. I didn't much like the surly American, but in a way I felt sorry for a fellow who didn't know how to get along without the artificial noises that properly belong to city life. Besides I was curious about young Ellwood. Why had he chosen to travel across this hot, lonely land, the

lonely, slow way when he could have gone to his new job in northwestern Australia by fast plane? It was certainly something of a mystery.

In the following week, Ellwood's selfishness became even more troublesome. At one moment he would be riding beside me, irritated by the blazing sun, and angry with his camel. Then, all of a sudden, he'd be gone. We'd ignore his absences for an hour or more, but in the end Peter would send Cooracardie or Tabalu in search of him.

Invariably our aboriginals found him and brought him back. At first Peter tried to reason with him, pointing out the dangers of getting lost in the bush. But when Ellwood ignored the warnings and continued his lone excursions, Peter tackled him less politely.

"This is *not* a little tourist trip," he told Ellwood. "You've been a downright danger to us. Because of you we've wasted time and that means we've wasted some of our supplies . . . our food. It's got to stop. From now on you'll ride in front of me where I can keep an eye on you."

Ellwood didn't trouble to apologize. He stomped away

and a few minutes later his tape-recorded pop music was shattering the peace of our night.

On the ninth day out from Ilara Homestead we reached Lake Mackay. Never had the sight of water thrilled me more. The five of us stripped and flung ourselves into the warm, bitter-tasting lake, enjoying the first good cleanup since the beginning of the trip. Later we settled down on the rocks at the edge of the water.

Cooracardie had just put on the kettle when Tabalu suddenly pointed to a distant rock. "Willy-willy!" he called.

"Shall we put out the fire?" asked Peter.

"No," said Tabalu, "he not pass here."

I had seen willy-willies from the air, but on land the thing looked even more astonishing. It was as if a pillar as tall as a church were leaping toward us at great speed. It was skipping and hopping and rushing round in circles like a crazy dancer.

"What is it?" asked Ellwood.

"A kind of sandstorm."

"But there's no wind."

"No," said Peter, "there's no wind. Willy-willies have their own built-in storm centers. If I were you I'd stay put and lie flat on the ground."

The camels were the first to go down, flattening their necks into the Spinifex grass. Then the rest of us lay down, all except Ellwood. He wandered off toward the column of sand, shielding his eyes against the sun.

I noticed that Cooracardie was watching him attentively, but without saying a word.

I felt the blast of hot air before the willy-willy was upon us. And then the light was blotted out. Sand swept over my head, through my hair, into my eyes and mouth. From Ellwood's direction came a yell of pain.

Before we could scramble to our feet, the willy-willy had passed and was leaping away into the distant east.

Ellwood was still lying prone on the ground, where the sandstorm had flung him down. He was gasping and choking as if someone had him by the throat. Cooracardie lifted his shoulders and put a mug of water to his lips. "You were lucky," he said. "It was only the edge of the willy-willy that hit you."

"Gee," spluttered Ellwood. "You mean that kinda storm can hurt you?"

"It can kill you," said Peter.

"Then why didn't you say so *before* I got knocked out?"

"Cooracardie was watching you."

"A lot of good that was."

"Sure. You aren't hurt, are you? Cooracardie knew exactly where the willy-willy was going to pass. He wouldn't have let you get into serious trouble."

"Just *trouble*," said Ellwood bitterly.

"I warned you."

Ellwood got up and shook himself. "That sand!" He spat, narrowly missing Tabalu. "It's gotten in everywhere."

The sand, we discovered that night, had gotten inside Ellwood's tape recorder. It was the finest of red dust, yet it had the most destructive effect on the pop singer's voice. When the tape didn't stick, cutting off the recording altogether, the sand scraped the tape, making it sound like tons of gravel being tipped off a lorry. Even Ellwood couldn't put up with the noise. He took the little machine to pieces, cleaned the parts with a handkerchief, unwound the tape, rewound it—all to no avail.

In the end he stowed away the tape recorder in his kit and sat down beside me at the campfire. Maybe Peter felt sorry for him—Ellwood was so obviously upset—because for the first time he and the aboriginal boys came to sit with us.

Cooracardie heated a stew, canned at Ilara, and shared it out into our billycans. We ate it with the *bread* Tabalu had made of flour and water. It was a big meal and the mugs of strong tea afterward were just right.

It was a beautiful night, with the stars so bright that I could pick out more constellations than I'd ever seen before —even from an airplane. And it was quiet—so quiet that I felt we'd arrived in a world outside our earth. The only sounds came from the camels; a soft stirring in the mulga grass as one of the animals would shift into a more comfortable position, a sigh, or perhaps a slight snore.

I was about to get inside my sleeping bag for the night when Ellwood blew his top.

"You guys dumb or somethin'?" Seemingly he could stand the silence no longer. By the light of the fire he looked nervous and unhappy. "Well—say somethin', can't you?"

"We've been listening," said Peter quietly.

"To the road traffic, I guess."

Peter ignored the sarcasm. "Listen."

It was several minutes before I caught the sound which Peter and the aboriginals had been hearing. It was hardly a sound—more a vibration in the air, a kind of beat one could feel rather than hear.

"What is it?" Ellwood sounded unsure of himself.

"A message," said Cooracardie.

"Drums?"

"Yes."

"There are *people* around?"

"My friends of the Kukatja tribe. Peter, we must go and speak with them."

About an hour after Cooracardie and Peter had left, the drumming stopped. Tabalu had gone to sleep, curled up beside the camels. And now the silence was complete—so perfect that the shifting of a grain of sand seemed as loud as an explosion. Nothing stirred except Ellwood, who'd neither go to sleep nor stop himself from listening into the night. He sat by the dying fire, hating the stillness, maybe hoping he'd hear *something*—Cooracardie and Peter returning, an animal, a bird, anything at all.

Finally I took pity on him. "You weren't to know what the bush is like," I said. "There are things about it that I didn't expect—though God knows I've seen it often enough from the air. Things like rocks that look . . . well, almost alive. Things like a night sky that looks no farther away than the ceiling in a room, or this queer absence of noises."

"Yeah . . . there's a whole lot I didn't expect. I guess it's one thing looking at a map and picking out a place you want to get to six hundred miles away . . . and quite another traveling such a distance through sand and heat—and this kinda quietness."

"What I can't understand is *why* you wanted to go with us."

"It's as good a way as any of spending the holiday I had coming to me."

I didn't believe Ellwood. His explanation, if one could call it that, just didn't ring true.

"Is *that* all?"

"Sure," he snapped. "It's useful for me to see this country," he added more mildly. "On account of my job . . . in case the company I'm going to work for opens up more mines in the future."

"Here, in the Center?"

"It's possible. Some of the mountains we passed look rich

in minerals. Mind you, I don't think there'll be any mining in the interior for years. It's a big scheme the Conzinc Rio Tinto Company's got going in the northwest. It'll keep busy all the men we can find for the next ten years or more."

"That's a long time ahead."

"Sure. Do you know, Mac, what it's like around Mount Tom Price? And all the way up the west coast as far as Dampierland?"

"I've read about it in the papers. A big new mine's been opened up, hasn't it?"

"You can say that again! A new mine! It's bigger than the gold rush of a hundred years ago. There's something like 17,000 million tons of the richest-known ore in the Hamersley Range . . . it's 67 per cent haematite . . . and that means big money. The companies which are mining the ore are spending one million pounds a week on equipment. Some of the guys who found the ore are going to be mighty rich . . . like the old-time prospectors Hildich and Warman. They're going to get one million pounds each. And Mr. Hancock, the grazier, will make about eight million pounds. Do you realize, Mac, that Australia will soon be making more money out of iron ore than out of the old wool trade?"

While Ellwood talked of his work I almost came to like him. Clearly he felt genuinely excited about the new mines; he certainly managed to make the whole project sound interesting. The very vastness of it made it seem like a great adventure. . . . the idea of huge hundred-ton lorries carrying the ore down four thousand feet high Mount Tom Price, the Japanese-built ore-crushing plant halfway down the mountain, the ore traveling on 179 miles of rail in trains of two hundred cars carrying one hundred tons each.

It was hard to believe, in the quiet of the bush, that some six hundred miles to the west, men were chopping up and carrying away whole mountains.

On the following nights I learned a lot more about the new mines. Ellwood told me of the new harbor which was being built at Kingbay-Dampier and about the enormous bunkers where the ore was to be stored. From the bunkers the ore was to travel over two miles of conveyor belts, at six thousand tons per hour, straight to the ships in the new harbor. The ships, gigantic 100,000-ton vessels, were to carry the ore to Japan. The Japanese steel mills expected 65½ million tons of Australian ore over the next sixteen years.

As Ellwood had said, Australia was on the way to becoming a wealthy country.

"Is that why you're here with us?" asked Peter one evening. "Is it because you want to know how much cash the mountains in the *interior* are worth?"

"Well, what's wrong with that?" asked Ellwood aggressively. "Do you want to keep this land a useless desert forever?"

"No, not useless. I want to see this country irrigated. I want water here so that there can be more farms, more cattle, kangaroo—above all—for the people who are the true natives of this country."

"Your pets, the abos?"

"My friends, the aboriginals."

"They can go work in the mines."

"*That* they can't and won't do."

"Too special, are they, for doing an honest day's work?"

"Yes, they *are* special people. And if you took them out of the life which has been theirs for thousands of years, you'd kill them."

"Okay, what *is* that life of theirs?"

"For one thing it's a nomadic life. . . . They're people who wander about the country. . . ."

"How do they live if not off the white farmers?"

"The true aboriginal is a hunter."

"A savage."

"On the contrary, a civilized human being who takes no more from nature than he needs to keep alive."

"If the abos are civilized, they've certainly managed to keep it secret from the rest of the world."

"Yes," said Peter. "They *are* a secret people."

Secret? I thought it was the right word for the aboriginals. On our way to Lake Disappointment, during the second part of our journey, I had the impression that we were being observed and followed—even when no one was in sight.

From time to time Cooracardie and Tabalu would dismount, examine a piece of ground, and confer with one another. But whatever information they discovered from the sands, it was invisible to me. Usually it was not until nightfall that single men would suddenly appear at our campfire. They'd talk with our two aboriginals and with Peter, accept a meal or just a mug of tea and vanish back into the bush.

After one such visit I asked Peter what these aboriginals wanted.

"It's *we* who want something of them," Peter explained. "We need scouts to guide us to Lake Disappointment. The aboriginals of this area are providing them. . . . We're now well outside Aranda territory. Even Cooracardie and Tabalu are strangers here. That's why they've asked the men of another tribe to help us."

"Are these guys *reliable?*" asked Ellwood.

"Of course. The men come from a tribe which is related to Cooracardie's Aranda."

Ellwood shrugged. "So what! It doesn't ensure that they

won't leave us stranded in the scorching sun . . . some place where no one will find as much as our dead bones."

"If you dislike aboriginals so much you shouldn't have come on this trip."

"I know nothing *about* abos."

"That's obvious. . . . Don't worry." Peter had mastered his irritation with the American. "You're in the hands of people who obey stricter rules than *you* have ever obeyed. And one of them is that aboriginal friends and relations make themselves responsible for one another's safety—especially in the bush."

In the furnace heat of the following day we reached Lake Disappointment. We had expected to find grazing for the camels, water for a swim, and the truck which was to take us to our destination—the mining camp of Mount Tom Price. We found none of it.

The lake was no more than a dried-up depression with a small water hole in the center. The country round about consisted of a wilderness of sharp red rocks, corrugated sand drifts, and a miserable scattering of mulga—tough swaths which didn't tempt even the modest appetite of a camel. Of all the dead, lonely places we had seen in the bush, this was the worst. Had anyone told me that no living creature had set eyes on the place for thousands of years, I'd have believed it. Yet someone must have found this spot within the past hundred years, someone who had given it the suitable name of Lake Disappointment.

About six in the evening, when the heat had become more bearable, a solitary camel appeared on the horizon. It shambled wearily into our camp and collapsed beside our animals. Its rider, a white-haired aboriginal, sat down with Cooracardie, Tabalu, and Peter. Paying no attention to

Ellwood and me, they all settled down to a long talk. And still there was no sign of the truck which should have been waiting for us.

Oddly enough, Ellwood showed none of his usual impatience. He stayed beside me, silent and motionless, and kept staring at the old aboriginal. He didn't take his eyes off the man.

When Peter joined us, a couple of hours later, he looked worried. "There must have been an accident," he said. "Our truck was last seen two days ago, about fifty miles from here. We'll have to help with the search. . . . Mac, I want you and Ellwood to stay here. You have enough food for three or four days."

"Say! You mean you're leaving us *alone?*" asked Ellwood. "Taking the abos with you?"

Despite his anxiety Peter smiled. "I'm also taking all the camels. . . . I need every man who knows the bush. And we'll have to move fast or the driver of the truck will be dead before we find him. He may be injured."

"You could leave us at least *one* of the abos," said Ellwood.

"Don't you ever think of anyone but yourself?" Peter turned on him. "Get *this* into your fat head. . . . Out there," Peter pointed into the stony desert, "a man's in bad trouble. He set out from Mount Tom Price because his boss had asked him to pick up a party in the bush. An unusual assignment. Knowing the bush, he maybe didn't fancy the job. But . . . off he goes. He drives some three hundred and fifty miles through the heat, the flies, through bull dust which can bog down any car. He has no map, because there isn't such a thing for this part of the world. . . . He drives with a compass and uses what experience he has. . . . Then, with the end of the journey in sight, something happens. . . . Perhaps the truck hit a submerged outcrop of rock. Or the water tank may have burst. Or the truck may have overturned in a creek. Whatever it is that's happened, it's bound to be dangerous for the driver. For all we know, he may have been lying injured in the sun . . . for *two* days. And believe me, in desert country like this the sun's a killer."

"Okay, okay," Ellwood was angry. "I guess you know all about looking for a needle in the haystack. What I don't get is why you have to leave *us* stranded in this Godforsaken place without as much as a . . ."

"I have no time to argue with you." Peter turned sharply. "Aluridja is waiting for me."

"Hey! Wait! Did you say that old abo's name's *Aluridja?*"

If I'd been left alone by the campfire I should have been contented. Maybe I'd have put on the battery lamp and read for a while in the Bible I'd taken along. Perhaps I'd just have listened to the silence. Silence *is* something one can listen to because it contains small noises that make one realize *how* quiet it is; the faint dry whisper of mulga, when the cooler air of night makes the grasses lift their blades from the sun-baked sands; the stirring of a sleeping lizard; the fall of a pebble.

But there was no peace with Ellwood beside me. Even when he wasn't scrabbling around in his kit or poking the fire, he somehow made me aware of his annoyance at being left behind. His pop music would have been better than this futile restlessness. Yet I felt sorry for the man. I wanted to help him out of his nervousness—distract his thoughts.

"What does *Aluridja* mean to you?" I asked him.

Ellwood's head lifted. "Why?"

"I'm asking *you*. I could see that the old aboriginal who came to tell Peter about the truck interested you. All along

you've paid no attention to Cooracardie and Tabalu . . .
except when you were rude to them. Yet you never took
your eyes off the old man who came tonight. And then you
asked Peter to repeat his name—or rather the name of his
tribe."

"Aluridja is the name of a tribe?"

"Yes. They're aboriginals of Western Australia. What do
you know about them?"

"Nothing."

"That's not true, is it?"

"No," admitted Ellwood after a while. "I once knew a
little guy who was called Aluridja. A long time ago."

"When you lived in Alice Springs as a boy?"

"Yeah."

"About ten years ago?"

"I guess so. That's when we left the States because my
father got appointed to the technical station at Alice. We
went by ship from San Francisco, my mother, Dad, and I.
I still remember the journey. We saw some great places. . . .
Hawaii," Ellwood grinned, "where I made myself sick eating
too many pineapples. . . . Japan . . . Hong Kong . . .
Manila. I liked the fast ball game they play there, like the
Spanish pelota. We landed in Sydney. Liked that too . . .
the fine harbor, the bridge, the people real friendly. They're
great guys, the Australians. . . . When we got to Alice
Springs they'd fixed up a bungalow for us . . . even a bunch
of flowers in the living room. Then . . . then . . . well . . .
after a while things went wrong. . . ."

Aluridja

THINGS DON'T USUALLY GO WRONG without a reason, not even for moody, complicated people like Billie Ellwood. I think the beginning of his troubles lay in the fact that he was plunged from the big, crowded city of Los Angeles into a quiet place no bigger than an English village.

By the time he was thirteen, when his family moved to the Center of Australia, he had become used to his school of five thousand boys, to long rides in big cars, to swimming in the Pacific Ocean, to baseball games and a choice of cinema and television programs.

Alice Springs offered him none of these things. The school was so small that all the boys and girls of his age knew him within days of his arrival. There was nowhere to go in a car except to one or two farms which were not too far from the little town. There was no baseball, no television, and only one cinema. And Billie had to do his swimming in a pool which seemed to him the size of a puddle.

The Ellwoods' bungalow was not exciting either. It consisted of four rooms, a kitchen, and a bathroom, enclosed by a veranda, with windows made of a fine wire netting. Outside, in the yard, there was a washhouse, shaded by a couple of gum trees, and a bedraggled flower bed of stunted roses, daisies, and cacti.

At midday, when the heat was pressing down on the bungalow, Billie liked to sit on the north side of the veranda and watch the people of Alice go home for their lunch, the shopkeepers of Todd Street, Police Sergeant Smith, Pastor Jonathan with an odd aboriginal from the mission and the kids from the high school.

When his mother called him he would gobble his meal without appetite and return to the veranda, particularly when his parents had visitors. He was not interested in the adults' talk; it usually centered around Australian politics or the problems of gardening. Mrs. Barber especially was full of advice on how the Ellwoods' could improve their yard.

One day, when Mrs. Barber had brought a box of plants, Billie listened to her voice until it sent him to sleep. When the rattle of a passing lorry aroused him, Mrs. Barber and his mother were still talking. Outside a hot wind was whipping up the red sand, driving it through the wire-net windows of the veranda and flinging the black bushflies at the washhouse wall. Billie wondered whether he should clean the dust off the chairs and the floor—to please his mother. But there seemed no point in it; while the wind kept swirling the sand, the dust would keep blowing inside.

He thought about going to the pool. The water would be all right. But the flies were a nuisance—the way they settled on you the moment you got out of the water. Was it worth going out? He was about to fetch his towel when he saw a movement in the yard. Something was hopping out from under the gum trees, something small and fluffy that looked like a flying powder puff.

In a flash Billie was out in the yard. Indifferent to the heat and the sand that blew into his eyes, he went in pursuit of the little creature. He rushed after it from end to end of the yard, but every time he came within touching distance, it took off again with a mighty leap which would have been right for a wallaby, but looked ridiculous for a creature so small.

Billie realized that he'd have to change his tactics. He sauntered over into the shade and leaned against one of the gum trees. For a while the animal continued its flight around the yard, but in the end it settled down at the edge of the flower bed. What Billie saw was something like a supermouse . . . about twice the size of an ordinary mouse, but with beautiful long ears and a fine bushy tail. The striking thing about the animal was that its hind legs were at least twice as long as its forelegs, so that its figure resembled a kangaroo's. A miniature kangaroo with the head of a mouse, the ears of a rabbit, and the tail of a squirrel.

It was like something out of a dream. Yet there it sat, sand-colored and silky and perfectly at ease.

Billie pounced, and missed. By the time he'd straightened up the supermouse was sitting on the shoulder of a grinning aboriginal boy.

The aboriginal gently removed the animal from its perch and handed it to Billie. "Him dargawarra."

"Gee, what's *that*?"

"I," the dark boy pointed at himself, "Aluridja."

"Your name?"

"Yes, Aluridja. . . . You say *Ali*."

"Okay, Ali. . . . What kinda animal's this?"

"Is dargawarra."

"I guess I don't know what you mean."

"Come."

As the aboriginal boy moved toward the gate, the super-mouse in Billie's hand began to struggle. Kicking and wriggling, it managed to free itself, leap into the air, and land on Ali's shoulder.

"Him is me, me is him," said Ali. "You come."

Billie followed boy and mouse into the road. Ali led him down Hartley Street and turned left at the last house. They crossed a patch of open ground, walked down a lane, and came upon a neat bungalow with a show window. It was so far from the shopping streets that the sight of it surprised Billie. Even more unusual was the bungalow's little front garden with its profusion of flowers. It was astonishing that such a variety of roses, pinks, and tropical plants could live and flower in the heat of Alice Springs.

Ali gave a low whistle and almost at once a white-haired aboriginal appeared on the path at the side of the bungalow.

"He garden man," said Ali. And then he continued to

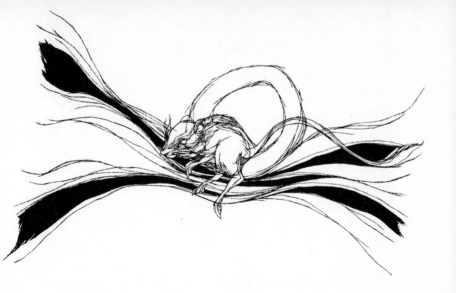

talk in a language Billie had never heard before.

The old gardener listened, nodding his head, smiling at Billie. He caressed the little animal on Ali's shoulder with one finger of his horny hand.

"He know," Ali announced at last.

"What?"

"Name of dargawarra."

"Yes," said the gardener. "Dargawarra is *our* name for animal. White man call him kangaroo mouse."

Billie thanked the old man. He'd meant to ask what the kangaroo mouse fed on, whether kangaroo mice could be bought in Alice, how long they lived, and a whole lot of other questions. What made him forget, quite suddenly, was the sight of the objects in the bungalow's show window.

What Billie saw some ten yards away distracted him so much that he lost interest in Ali's pet. He wanted to be left alone. But the only way to achieve that was to accompany Ali back to where they'd met.

Ali, on the other hand, had adopted Billie as a new friend and was chattering away, telling Billie that he lived on Mrs. Barber's homestead, that his father worked there as a stockman, and that Mrs. Barber sometimes took them into Alice in her car.

"I come see you again," he promised. "With dargawarra."

"Okay," said Billy, without much interest.

Back at the Ellwoods' bungalow Mrs. Barber was waiting beside her car. "Ali, where have you been?" she asked.

"Go talk with uncle," Ali told her.

"All right. Hop in. Hurry up, boy." She waved to Billie's mother. "Never take a fellow like this with you when you're pressed for time. I suppose I'm lucky he hasn't gone walkabout." The car made off in a cloud of red dust.

"Billie, why aren't you at the pool?" asked Mrs. Ellwood.

Billie dived past her into the house. "I'm just going, Mum."

He went off with trunks and towel, but he didn't go swimming. He returned to the bungalow with the show window. For a while he hung around at the open garden gate. When he was sure that no one was in sight, not even Ali's uncle, he quietly made his way along the path right up to the window.

Now many more of the stones displayed on black velvet were in sunlight. He had never seen such colors. There were milky-white stones with specks of gold and orange that seemed to flicker like tiny flames. There were stones of a blue so vivid that staring at them made his eyes water. There were crystals enclosing round stones of an intense red or a near black; yet behind the black and the red, Billie could see blue and amber lights which seemed on the point of bursting through to the surface.

As Billie stood with his face pressed against the window, he remembered the stories he'd read as a small child— about pirate ships, the gold of the Incas, about lost and found treasure. But what *was* treasure if not these stones before him, these crystals with flames imprisoned inside them?

From that day Billie visited *his* stones as one would visit a friend. When no one was about, he'd stay for a long time. If there were visitors, he'd slip behind some bushes at the side of the bungalow and leave the garden through a hole in the fence.

No one but Ali knew of his treasure, or rather of the pleasure its existence gave him. And even Ali wouldn't have known if he hadn't surprised Billie at the window one day when he was looking for his uncle.

"What you doing?" Ali asked.

"I kinda like these rocks," Billie had told him.

Ali had gazed at him with something like surprise. "Cacholong."

"Cacholong?"

"Is name for stones. . . . I bring you cacholong."

After that Ali had come into Alice with a variety of pebbles—rusty red, green, white with gray veins. "You like?" he'd ask.

"It's great," Billie would assure him.

But Ali always knew that he hadn't found the right thing. He'd go away promising, "I bring you cacholong."

Toward Christmas the heat in Alice became almost unbearable. While Billie's mother debated with herself whether the family would be able to eat turkey in such a climate, while Billie's father kept coming home for cold showers, and while the grass shriveled up in the gardens of Hartley Street, Billie continued to visit his treasure.

One day, as he was gazing at a new stone, someone touched his shoulder. He flinched. He tried to make off, but the old woman who had found him held on to his arm.

"Don't go," she said pleasantly. "You have a right to look at our stones. This is a shop, you know. What's your name?"

"Billie Ellwood."

"I've seen you here before. . . . How would you like to come in? The best of Mrs. Jenkins' stones are inside. You know, Mrs. Jenkins has one of the finest collections of opals in the world. You'd like to see it, wouldn't you?"

"Sure," muttered Billie.

In the bungalow all the doors were open and Billie could see into rooms with vases of flowers and chintz-covered chairs which looked as friendly as his aunt's home in New England. But there were also the showcases, and Billie made straight for the collection of stones.

"I don't suppose you want to wait for a cup of tea," said Miss Pitt. She opened a cupboard and took out a bottle of orange squash and some glasses. "We'll just have a cold drink."

"Thanks. . . . What's this?" Billie pointed to the largest of the milky stones with flecks of yellow and red.

"It's called hyalite."

"And this one?"

"Ah, it's one of the finest opals we have . . . a girasol or fire opal. It comes from a place called Lightning Ridge. . . . Here, no reason why you shouldn't see it properly." Miss Pitt opened the glass door of the showcase, took out the stone, and handed it to Billie. "Here's a magnifying glass. . . . That's better, isn't it? Have you ever seen such colors?"

"Gee, it's . . . it's better than gold."

Miss Pitt laughed. "It also costs more than gold. It's rare, very rare that a stone like this is mined."

"Mined?"

"Yes. People look for opals the same way as they did for

gold. They make shafts in the rock and burrow inside mountains."

"Can't you . . . just find an opal?"

"On the surface? Sometimes. But that's most unusual."

"What does cacholong mean?"

"Oh, that's what the aboriginals call opals. It means beautiful stone. . . . What are *you* doing here?" Miss Pitt's face hardened at the sight of the man who had shambled into the shop. Small as she was, she managed to look almost fierce. "Sailor, Mrs. Jenkins has told you more than once you're not to bother us."

"Now, don't take on, Miss Pitt." The man, a skinny figure in ragged cotton trousers and a grubby shirt, came closer. "Mrs. Jenkins wouldn't thank you if you missed out on a real gem of a stone, would she?"

"I've heard *that* story before."

"But this is different, Miss Pitt. This time I ain't drunk. . . . See here, you can't say I'm drunk. . . ."

"I'm not saying you are. But you soon will be, if I know you."

"If you're down on your luck people treat you lousy," whined the man. "It's always the same."

"Oh, for goodness' sake! If you *have* something to show me, let me see."

The man produced a rag from his pocket and put it on the glass counter. He fumbled with shaking hands. "Here! What d'you say now? Ever seen a finer stone?" He put it in Miss Pitt's open palm. "Well?"

Held to the light between her thumb and index finger, the ordinary-looking brown pebble revealed a smooth spot a quarter of an inch long and about half as wide. "Could be," murmured Miss Pitt. "Yes, it's possible."

"It's a fire opal all right. You can bet your life."

"It could also be a black opal. . . ."

"Look, Miss, you know it's a good one, so don't pretend
it ain't." The sailor leaned across the counter. "What'll you
give me, eh?"

"*I* can't give you anything," said Miss Pitt. "First of all
the stone will have to be properly examined. If it's good
Mrs. Jenkins will decide the price."

"Oh no, Miss, it's me what's going to decide the price."

"Sorry, Sailor, that's not how we do business. If the
stone's worth having, you'll get a fair offer."

"Look, Miss, I don't want to be unreasonable. . . . Tell
you what; you give me a fiver and . . ."

"Sorry, I can't."

"Only five pounds, Miss. And I'll leave the stone. . . ."

"No good. If you want to sell come back tomorrow
when Mrs. Jenkins is here."

"No, I ain't coming back!" shouted the sailor. "Mrs.
Jenkins ain't the only one what buys opals. Well, you giving
me a fiver?"

"No."

"You'll be sorry, you old cat!" The tramp wrapped up his
stone stuffed it into his pocket and stomped out. At the
door he turned, "Call yourself a business, do you?"

"Don't make trouble, Sailor. I don't want to have to call
the police again." Miss Pitt watched until the man was out
of the front garden. "Sorry, Billie. . . . He's a poor old man
really."

"Why didn't you give him the money?"

"Five pounds is no good to him. He just goes and gets
drunk. Then he gets into fights and the police have to run
him in. . . . It's not his fault entirely. Just . . . well, the
bush has been too much for him. For every man who's gone

looking for opals and found enough to live on, there are
dozens who have become tramps like poor old Sailor."

"But the stone he showed you . . . wasn't it any good?"

"Maybe, but only an expert would know for sure. A
stone that size could be cracked . . . or have other blemishes
that ruin its value. . . . Don't worry about the sailor,
Billie. *He'll* be back."

The sailor was sitting under the only gum tree on the
rough patch of ground at the end of Hartley Street. He
looked like a discarded bundle of rags.

"Got a bob for a thirsty old seaman?" he asked Billie.
"It's a hard life in this heat, sonny."

Billie searched his pockets. He found some pennies and a
six pence and gave them to the sailor. "Would you . . ." his
heart was beating fast, "would you sell your stone to *me?*"

"To *you?*" A dry cackling noise came from the sailor's
toothless mouth. The bloodshot eyes screwed up. "Well . . .
well . . . so the little gentleman's gone overboard for
opals. . . . My, my! Who'd believe it . . . a young lad like
you getting hooked on stones. . . . What'll you give me for
my fine fire opal, eh?"

"I guess I got about ten pounds saved up."

"A lot of money. You an American?"

"Yes."

"Maybe your dad would like to buy the stone?"

"I don't think so. . . . Can't I . . ."

"Sonny, that stone's worth a hundred times your ten
pounds. If your father . . ."

"But you don't *know* what it's worth. It's got to be
examined," Billie rushed on, "and if it's cracked or it's got
flaws . . ."

"Flaws!" shouted the sailor. "My stone . . . flaws!" He
scrambled to his feet. "You little stinker! *You* want to do

business with me! *You!*" He lunged at Billie. "I'll teach you. . . ."

Billie twisted out of the sailor's grip and ran. His face streaming with sweat, he raced up Hartley Street. He knew the sailor wasn't following him, yet he couldn't bring himself to walk as if nothing had happened. But what *had* happened? Why had the sailor been so angry? Had it been wrong to want to buy the stone? Was it wrong to *want* such a stone?

Ali didn't see anything strange in Billie's liking for stones. A few days before Christmas he came with another of his gifts.

"Cacholong . . . for you."

Billie examined the green pebble the aboriginal boy had given him. "Thanks, Ali."

"You no like." The dark head bowed, sadly. "No cacholong."

"Sure, Ali, it *is* a beautiful stone."

"For me, *all* stone beautiful. For you, no. . . . For *you* only dreamtime cacholong."

"What's dreamtime stone?"

"I bring."

"Ali, it's okay."

"No."

"Look." Billie put his arm round Ali's shoulders, making the kangaroo mouse leap on Ali's head. "You come along with me. I'll show you." He led Ali up the veranda steps and into his room. "See?"

The stones Ali had given him were set out on a shelf above his books. They were colorful pebbles. There was a gray rock flecked with silver, but even that didn't have the deep-down fire of the crude stone the sailor had shown Miss Pitt.

Ali examined the pebbles, pleased to see them on display. But after a while he shook his head. "Is no cacholong for *you*."

"Gee, I *like* your rocks."

"No . . . for you is only dreamtime cacholong."

The next time Billie saw his aboriginal friend it was at Walillya Homestead where Mrs. Barber had invited the Ellwoods' for Boxing Day.

After tea Ali took him to the compound where the stockmen and their families lived in low, tin-roofed houses round a yard full of busy people. Aboriginal girls were building a pyramid of firewood, boys were polishing saddles and mending harnesses, and an old man was practicing with a stock whip.

Flicking the short, leather-covered handle of the whip with an easy movement of the wrist, the old man sent the twenty-five- or thirty-foot-long tail spiraling into the air with a sharp hiss. Then, very gently, the tail descended and coiled neatly round the trunk of a dead gum tree.

"Father of father Aluridja," Ali introduced Billie and the old man. "You want whip?"

The grandfather gave Billie the stock whip. "Like this." He guided Billie's wrist. . . . "Slow, slow. Is dangerous for new man."

It had looked easy, but it wasn't. Billie managed to whip up dust and to tie the tail round his own body. In the end he had to be satisfied with a throw which at least got the tail well off the ground.

"Aluridja is best with whip," said Ali. "This night you see."

That night the aboriginals of Walillya Homestead staged a big corroboree. The display of skills with the stock whip was just a small part of the celebrations. There was dancing around the great bonfire. There was singing to the accompaniment of drums which were hollow tree trunks. And there was a kind of theater performance in which the aboriginals acted scenes of their life on the farm and mimed the ways of the white owners. The Barbers and Billie's parents joined in the laughter and enjoyed themselves as much as the aboriginals.

It was after midnight when Mr. Barber showed Billie to his room. Still wide-awake, Billie lay on his back and listened to the drumbeats and the singing. The party was going on without the white people. From his bed he could see a square of sky, rose tinted by the fire, and the passing shadow of a horseman.

"Billie."

He leaped up and went to the window. Through the fly net he saw someone on horseback, peering in. "Ali?"

"Is me. You come."

"What? Now?"

"Now. . . . We go ride on horse quick."

When Billie later tried to remember that night, it was as unclear as a dream, a jumble of impressions that did not add up to any kind of sensible experience. He could not have told anyone what had happened, yet single moments of these early-morning hours stayed in his mind like poems he'd been made to learn by heart and could not forget.

There was the extraordinary brightness of the stars, the strong silvery light in which he could see every bush, every fissure in the tall rocks. There was Ali's figure on the horse in front of him. He'd clung to Ali, afraid of falling off. Or perhaps he'd been frightened of other things—the speed of the horse, the ever-more distant sound of the drums.

Then they'd been scrambling up a rock face. And suddenly Ali had disappeared. He'd been left alone on a small ledge with the dead silent night about him. After a long time, Ali and he had crept through a cave. At the end of a passage they'd come upon a rock chamber as tall as a barn.

There had been drawings on the walls—patterns, faces, shapes like boomerangs. And Ali had kept talking of *dreamtime* and an ancient *hero* to whom the cave belonged. Billie had understood very little except that Ali—who had *not* been afraid of riding through the night—was extremely frightened in the cave.

The flashlight had trembled in Ali's hand, yet the fingers of his free hand had wandered over the walls until they had found the loose rock—a cavity, some teeth inside, sharp objects, stones.

The *dreamtime cacholongs.*

Ali had demanded that he choose one for himself.

Billie had refused.

They'd argued.

Much later Billie *had* taken a stone; he'd wanted to be out of that cave, out of the terrible moonlit stillness, back among people.

The stone from the cave had a smooth side the size of a halfpenny. When Billie let the sun shine on it, the circle glowed like embers on the verge of bursting into flame. Deep down, beneath the surface, flickered specks of gold and scarlet and peacock blue. The stone was a true cacholong.

During the burning days before the New Year, Billie spent most of his time in his room. The cacholong was on the shelf with his other pebbles; but when the sun reached his window in the afternoon he'd take it down and let it *catch fire*.

Two or three days after their return from Walillya Homestead, Billie heard his parents on the veranda.

"What's the matter with the boy?" asked his father.

"I think he's feeling the heat," said his mother.

"It's not like him to stay in his room."

"It's about the coolest place in the house."

"Maybe, Mary. But what's he doing with himself all day long?"

"He's got himself a big book out of the library—on rocks. Haven't you noticed? He's started collecting stones."

"Yes, I've seen his shelf. One or two of his pebbles look quite unusual. . . . Oh, well, if it's just a new hobby that's keeping him quiet . . ."

Billie took the opal off the shelf. The cacholong was *his*. He put it under his pillow. Yes, the stone belonged to him—at least for the moment.

On December 31, the Ellwoods gave a New Year's Eve party. To the sounds of recorded American-folk songs, Billie and a few of his schoolmates helped with the serving of chicken Maryland and cool drinks. The veranda was crowded with friends the Ellwoods had made and a few Americans from the technical base.

Around eleven o'clock, Billie and his mother went to the kitchen for fresh supplies of fruit cup. Filling the jug he was holding, his mother listened to the laughter on the veranda. "They're enjoying themselves."

"Sure," said Billie.

"It's amazing when you think of it. . . . Some of the

men out there are running a piece of Australia the size of France and Germany put together. Yet they're such simple, friendly people . . . the doctor, Pastor Jonathan . . ."

As they returned to the party Inspector Grayson arrived.

"Sorry I'm late, Mrs. Ellwood," he apologized. "New Year's a busy time for a policeman."

"Usual trouble?" asked the doctor.

"No," Inspector Grayson shook his head. "Oddly enough the pubs have been quiet. So far, no drunks."

The doctor laughed. "What? New Year's without a fight?"

"Oh, there's been a *fight*. The sailor's back in town."

"Poor old devil. He's in jail, I suppose."

"Afraid so." The inspector took the glass Billie's father was offering him. "Thanks, Mr. Ellwood. . . . This fellow we're talking about . . . he's mad about opals. He used to be a seaman. Turned up here forty years ago and stayed . . . like a lot of men who think they can get rich fast. He kept prospecting for opals. Sometimes he did find a stone —which was thoroughly unlucky for him because it kept him in the bush, hoping for more. Now . . . well, he's just an old tramp who gets drunk whenever someone's silly enough to give him money instead of food."

"What's he been up to this time?" asked the doctor.

"Picking a fight with Mrs. Jenkins' gardener. Says he's been robbed of an opal that's worth a fortune."

"One never knows," the doctor said, thoughtfully, "whether the sailor's imagining the things he tells people or whether he's just an old rogue."

"Well, this time he isn't lying. Miss Pitt says he did come into the shop with an opal. And he certainly hasn't got it now."

"He must have given it to someone to get money for drink."

"That's what *I* thought," agreed the inspector. "But it isn't so. The sailor did have money on him. . . . He got a pound out of his old chum Smith. He didn't give Smith the opal though; we checked on that. . . . It's a strange business."

"Mrs. Jenkins' gardener wouldn't rob anyone."

"Quite. The sailor thinks so too—now that he's almost sober. His latest statement is that it's a kid who took the opal. Says he went to sleep up at the Stuart Memorial and when he came to there was a boy beside him. . . ."

Billie felt a wave of heat rise from his throat into his face. And his father was watching him.

He said, "Go to your room, Bill."

The cacholong lay in Mr. Ellwood's outstretched palm. "This *is* an opal, isn't it?"

Billie nodded.

"Where did you get it?"

Billie stared at the stone, his eyes blurring with tears. What was he to say? He knew he shouldn't have gone into the bush that night. He knew that Ali had been wrong in taking the opal from the cave, and he knew he shouldn't have accepted it. Yes, Billie knew he was in the wrong, but he didn't really understand why.

"Well? I've asked you where you got this opal."

Billie made himself look at his father. "It *isn't* the one the sailor had. . . . It *isn't*."

"I see. So you *know* the sailor. And you know that he *had* an opal."

If Billie had tried to speak then he'd have burst into tears. How *could* his father think that he'd rob an old man? Yet . . . he *had* allowed Ali to rob. And he *had* accepted the stone.

"Billie," his father spoke more gently. "Don't you understand? This is very, very serious. A poor old man has been robbed of a gem stone for which he could probably have bought a place to live in and enough food for the rest of his life. You have just such a stone right here. Don't you see? I *must* know where you got this stone."

"Sure."

"Well, son?"

"Ali . . . he gave it to me."

Mr. Ellwood frowned. "What? The aboriginal boy?"

"Yes." Billie saw that his father didn't believe him. "We went . . . There was a cave. . . . We found it there. . . ."

"When?"

"On Boxing Day."

"On Boxing Day? When we were at Walillya Homestead?"

"Yes."

"And where *is* this cave?"

"I guess about five miles away."

"Five miles from the homestead?"

"I . . . I don't know. Maybe it's . . ."

"You *don't know*. Very well, then I'll tell *you*. You didn't go *half a mile* from the homestead, let alone five miles." Mr. Ellwood's hand closed on the opal. "All right, I've given you your chance." He went to the door and removed the key. "I'm not going to listen to any more of your lies. I'm going to give this stone to Inspector Grayson. And you'd better make up your mind to tell *him* the truth."

The key turned in the lock. Billie was alone. He no longer felt like crying. His father had *not* given him a chance. And if his father hadn't believed him, Inspector Grayson wouldn't believe him either. So *he* wasn't going to stay locked in . . . wait for them to put him in prison for something he hadn't done. He'd *prove* to them that he hadn't stolen the sailor's opal. He'd *get* the proof.

It didn't matter that his father had locked the door; he could not have got out that way because it opened to the side of the veranda where the party was going on. Billie went to his window and leaned out. Stacked chairs below. A dim light. The back door leading to the wash house and the yard. To reach the back door he'd have to pass the end of the well-lit part of the veranda. Someone might see him go across. But there was no better way.

As he climbed out of the window, the radio clock began to strike. Midnight. The New Year. Billie jumped on to the veranda and hid behind the chairs. People had stopped talking; only the clock was booming . . . on and on. Nine. Ten. Eleven. . . . On the stroke of twelve a man's voice rang out, "Happy New Year! A happy New Year to you all!"

"Happy New Year!" Other voices joined in. There was a tinkling of glasses, a sudden burst of talk and laughter.

Billie, looking cautiously round the corner, saw the guests crowded about his parents in a tight knot. They were drinking a toast to the New Year.

No one saw him leave the bungalow.

He left his bicycle at the very end of the town, where the last shack of an abandoned slum had been engulfed by the sands of the bush.

He walked on into the starlit night, passing clumps of silvery ghost gums, crossing stretches of hard-packed corrugated sand; walking, walking toward the distant peaks of rocks whose shapes he remembered.

Everything would be all right once he reached the homestead. He'd explain to Ali the trouble he was in. Then he'd telephone his father. His father and Inspector Grayson would come to Walillya and Ali would show them the cave of the *Dreamtime Hero* where they'd found the cacholongs.

Toward dawn he lay down and slept for a while. And when he wakened it was to the cries of the galahs, a flock of birds which rose into the sun like a pink cloud. He ate one of the apples he'd stuffed into his pocket and walked on, turning often to look for any car or truck that might give him a lift.

By midday he began to wonder just how often trucks did pass this way. Throughout the morning there hadn't been a sound. The uninterrupted silence began to worry him. The flies, the black bushflies which kept crawling over his face and over every bare part of his body worried him. He no longer recognized the shapes of the rocks. And the sun was burning down, pressing him down like a pair of heavy hands.

The sun was still high, still engulfing him in an unbearable furnace heat, when he dropped to the ground incapable of moving another step. Sand, rocks, flies were swimming before his eyes.

He fought off the flies. Then he clung to his opal. . . . Someone was trying to take his cacholong. Ali would help him. He tried to shout to Ali, but no sound was coming from his throat. Someone was squeezing his throat. They were strangling him. And then there was a moment when he *knew* what was happening to him. He was *imagining* that the opal was still his. He was *imagining* that Ali was near him. He was *imagining* that someone was trying to kill him.

There was no need for anyone to kill him. The sun would do it. The sun *was* doing it.

Weeks later, or so it seemed to Billie, he awakened. By

the dim light of a shaded lamp he recognized his room, his books, the stones on the shelf above the books. An electric fan had been fixed above his bed and was blowing cool air on his face. He felt no pain. Not even in his eyes. He was tired, just tired.

"Billie." His mother was kneeling beside him, holding his hand to her cheek. "Billie . . . look at me."

Billie looked, and wondered why his mother was looking so upset. "Hi, Mum."

"Hi, Billie." A tear spilled from her eyes. "You *know* where you are, son?"

"Sure I know."

"Where, Billie?"

"Gee . . . in my room." There was a gap among the stones on his shelf. "Mum, where is it?"

"What?"

"The opal."

"Don't you worry about it, Billie."

"Mum, I want to know."

"It's gone back where it belongs."

"I *didn't* . . . I *didn't* take the sailor's . . . It wasn't me. . . ."

"Billie, listen! We *know* you didn't take the sailor's opal. Miss Pitt told us. Your stone was quite different from the one the sailor lost."

"Who took it?"

"Inspector Grayson says *no one* took the sailor's stone. It must have fallen out of his pocket while he slept at the Stuart Memorial. It must have got lost in the sand."

"They didn't find it?"

"No, Billie."

"Sure . . . things get lost in the sand." The air was cool on his face, like the air at home—in the mountains of California. He let himself go back to sleep.

Night

THE GLOW OF THE CAMPFIRE lit Bill Ellwood's face. He was staring at the man-shaped outlines of the rocks beyond Lake Disappointment.

"So that's what happened, Mac," he said. "I figure the bush darned nearly killed me."

"Odd. If you knew how dangerous it is to run about the bush on your own, why the devil did you keep doing it on *this* trip?" There was no getting away from it—Bill Ellwood had been a nuisance to Peter and the rest of us on the first part of our journey. "Why did you take chances like that?"

"Gee, I didn't get lost."

"You *would* have got lost for sure if Cooracardie and Tabalu hadn't kept tracking you."

"Okay, I know. I'm sorry, Mac. Truly I am. It was just that . . . well, we passed certain rock formations which looked kinda familiar to me."

"You got the feeling you'd seen them when you were a boy?"

"That's right. . . . Times on this trip I figured I was seeing the ledge where Ali'd left me alone that night . . . before he found the entrance to the cave. All my life I wanted to find that cave again."

"So *that's* why you came on this trip with us."

"Sure. . . . You see, they never believed me when I told them about the cave of the Dreamtime Hero. Anyway, my *parents* didn't. They thought I'd imagined the place. . . . Oh, they went looking for it, with Inspector Grayson—a real search party went out to Walillya Homestead, complete with aboriginal trackers. But they never located the cave."

"The Aluridjas at the homestead must have known where the cave was. Ali's people."

"Yeah . . . Ali and his people. They just made themselves scarce. They went walkabout. The thing I just never got was the *proof* I wanted, the proof of *where* my opal had come from. After they found me half-dead in the bush, Ali and his folks disappeared—all but one of them."

"It *wasn't* your own people who found you?"

"No. Sure, there were parties out looking for me. Airplanes too. But they didn't find me. What they told me later is that an aboriginal had carried me into the hospital in the middle of the night. He'd told the duty doctor I'd been found in the bush near Trephina Gorge. Then he'd run away. . . . I guess it could have been *any* aboriginal, but I'm kinda certain in my own mind that he was one of Ali's folks. I guess I *was* delirious by the time they found me, but there's one thing I do remember. I don't think *that's* something I dreamed. I remember that little animal of Ali's, the kangaroo mouse he called dargawarra. . . . I was lying there in the sand with the sun burning down on me. And the flies were driving me nuts—getting inside my mouth, crawling around my eyes. And then, all of a sudden the flies took off. It was good, real good . . . just the sun, and no more flies driving me crazy. The thing which had scared off the flies was that funny little supermouse leaping around me like a high-jump champion. . . . He was the last thing I saw before I came to in my own bed. . . . Ali I didn't see. Nor his folks. I never saw any of them again except the old stockman who'd shown me how to handle the whip."

"*He* must have known where the cave was."

"Inspector Grayson thought so too. The inspector told me that the tribe had left the old Aluridja behind so that he could return the opal to the place where it belonged. . . . Of course, the stockman denied all knowledge of the cave. All he'd say was that it must have been some *dreamtime* place."

"So Inspector Grayson gave the opal to the stockman."

"Is that what you'd have expected?"

"Yes, Bill. But then I knew Inspector Grayson well. That was before he was transferred to Perth. There was no white man in the Northern Territories administration who knew more about the aboriginals than he did. . . . I expect when the old stockman talked to the inspector about a *dreamtime* place, Grayson knew at once that the opal was a stone the Aluridjas regarded as sacred . . . a stone that came from a sacred place."

"Yes. But how could he have been so sure that the stockman wouldn't steal the opal? Sell it and keep the money for himself?"

"Grayson *was* certain?"

"Yes. That's the funny part of it."

"Not as funny as you think—for two reasons. Firstly, Grayson knew that one of the most important laws of the aboriginal tribes is that *all* belongings are shared by families and tribes. It's very rare for an aboriginal to keep something of value to himself—to break the rule, in fact. Secondly, you say the aboriginals of Walillya Homestead disappeared into the bush leaving behind one man only—the stockman. To a man like Grayson, who understands these people, it must have been perfectly clear that Ali's people had left behind the most important man of their tribe—the headman."

"You mean they'd entrusted to him the task of recovering their opal?"

"*And* of returning it to the cave."

It was almost two o'clock in the morning, but neither Bill Ellwood nor I felt sleepy. We sat on by the fire, listening to the drums which were still beating softly and deeply through the night. Sometimes the beats were as even as the spatter of raindrops on a tin roof. Sometimes the rhythm would change to a fast rattle interspersed with long pauses.

"Will they keep it up all night?" asked Bill.

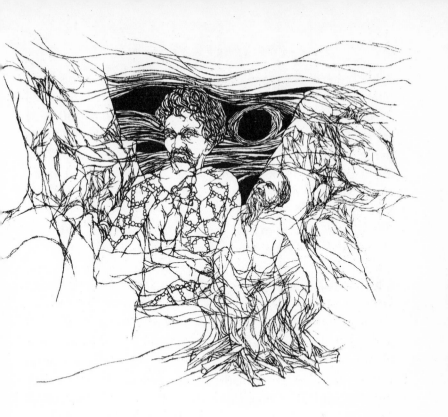

"I don't know. It depends."

"On the truck?"

"Or some trace of the truck that you or I wouldn't be able to see. . . . I think they're using the drums to keep in touch with Cooracardie, Tabalu, and Peter."

"When do you think they'll be back?"

"Your guess is as good as mine. You can be sure of one thing—you won't see them again until they've discovered what's happened to the truck."

"That could take *days*." It sounded like the old Ellwood, the fellow who wasn't worried about anyone, provided *he* was comfortable.

"Don't upset yourself," I said, none too friendly. "What if the search does go on for days and nights? *You'll* be all

right. You've got your shady spot under the rocks . . .
food . . . water. *You* won't suffer."

"Gee, Mac! Don't get me wrong. I was thinking of those
poor guys out there, covering miles and miles in the heat,
trying to find something in the bush . . . one little thing
like a truck in a country *this size*. . . . Look here, I don't
blame you for taking me for a guy who considers no one
but himself. . . ."

"If you're *not* then you certainly *behaved* like that kind
of fellow . . . playing that tape recorder of yours whether
the rest of us liked it or not . . . wandering off into the
bush on your own. . . ."

"I explained that."

"You did. But all the same it's no excuse. You gave
Peter and the aboriginal boys a bad time. And only a few
hours ago, when Peter took the aboriginals and the camels
off on the search, you made a fuss because Peter wouldn't
leave Tabalu or Cooracardie behind to look after you."

"You're right, Mac. I know. I guess Peter just rubbed me
up the wrong way . . . behaving as if he knew all there was
to know . . . the abo language, the bush. Look how he
handles Cooracardie and Tabalu. . . ."

"*I* wouldn't say he *handles* them. There's an understand-
ing between them. They . . ."

"I figured that out fast enough," interrupted Bill. "The
abos and he *belong* together. But he didn't have much time
for *me*, did he?"

"Because you behaved like a stinker, not least toward
Peter's aboriginal friends. But that's only a part of it. Part
of a misunderstanding. You see, Cooracardie, Tabalu, and
Peter are very old friends. When we set out from Mount
Isa, Peter was looking forward to this trip with them. He
hadn't seen them for several years. Wasn't it natural that

he should be more interested in them than in you or me? I too have known Peter since he was a kid, but I don't flatter myself that I'm as important to him as a friend as Cooracardie is."

"Maybe I'd understand better what you're getting at if I knew something *about* Peter . . . especially about how he got to know his aboriginals."

"Well, that's a story I can tell you. Because it happened just after I'd met Peter. As a matter of fact it was me who picked them up at Mount Isa—Peter and his father, Mr. Landson, just arrived from England. They'd come to visit their relations at Ilara Homestead. So I flew them over to Alice Springs. . . ."

I threw some more sticks on the fire. It was going to be a long story. *Quite* a story. I thought some of the things that had happened to Peter would explain to Bill Ellwood what *he'd* never understood; the meaning of *dreamtime*, the ways of those gentle black people who live among us one day and are gone the next, people who go *walkabout* —returning time and again to a faraway secret life which very few white people have ever been allowed to share.

Peter *was* one of the few. And Ellwood, though he himself couldn't yet see it, had returned to the bush because he *wanted* to be one of the few. I reckoned the best way of showing young Ellwood exactly what had happened to Peter, was to describe the whole thing to him just as Peter and Anita had described it to me after I'd taken part in the air search for Mr. Landson.

Cooracardie

T HE HEAD CREPT FORWARD, slowly, close to the ground.
The eyes, wide open, kept staring at Peter. They were old
eyes, as notice taking as Minu's. And like Minu, the aboriginal stockman on Anita's farm, the creature out there seemed

to have plenty of time for staring. And it was blocking the only exit from the cave.

Anita raised herself on her elbows, shifting the sharp, red pebbles. "You could . . ."

"Quiet," Peter warned her in a voice no louder than the lisping of the Spinifex grass.

He knew now what he should be doing. Slide backward into the dark, then lift an arm slowly, very slowly until he could grasp that head with the ancient eyes. . . .

But those eyes spoiled things. They kept looking at Peter as if he couldn't be expected to make any move. The creature lay as quietly as the flame-red rocks beyond the cave, as still as the pools of sand and the silver-white trunk of the decaying gum tree. Sleepily, Peter wondered whether it would be any use trying to catch whatever it was. Maybe it would be like taking hold of those blue flowers that felt like straw and crumbled to dust in one's hand. Maybe he'd finish up with nothing—just hotter and more thirsty than he was now.

"Ooff!" Anita had pounced at the creature's neck. She was pulling it into their cave.

The lizard was bigger than Peter had imagined—almost two feet long. But it was not putting up a fight. It had turned on its back and was pawing the air like a trustful puppy.

"Let him go, Anita."

"Peter, we've got to have something to eat."

"He may be poisonous."

"The aboriginals eat lizard."

"How do you know? Have you seen it?"

"No." Anita relaxed her hold on the lizard without letting go of its neck. "But everyone knows. The aboriginals who live in the bush have got to live on *something*."

"Kangaroos and grass seed . . . that's what Minu told me."

"Lizards too. Kangaroos are scarce here. We'll cook him."

"How?"

"Make a fire. Here . . ." She took a small leather wallet from the back pocket of her jeans. It held a comb and a mirror. "You collect dry sticks. There's ghost gums below the cave. Then you let the sun strike the mirror and shine it on to the sticks."

"Yes, I know about that. But I don't want to eat . . . well, animals one shouldn't eat."

"Don't be a coot, Peter. Australia isn't like England. In a country like this you've got to take what you can find or you die of hunger—especially when you're bushed."

"You said we *weren't* lost."

"Well," Anita gazed at the lizard, which was pretending to be dead. "I thought I knew this mountain."

"And you don't?"

"No. I suppose we should have stayed by the car."

"Walking was *your* idea."

"All right, Peter. It was. And I should have known better. . . . Well, do we cook the lizard?"

"I expect we have to."

Anita pushed it across. "*You* kill him."

As Peter took hold of the dry, warm body, wondering what to do with it, the lizard began to wiggle, its tail beating the pebbles. It looked good-natured and playful—not the kind of animal one wanted to hurt.

Suddenly Peter felt as if a rock had come crashing down on his arm. His wrists were crushed tight in the grip of thin, extremely strong fingers.

The attacking hands were as black as Minu's. Peter had

to let go of the lizard, and it immediately shot out of sight. Instead there appeared the face of an aboriginal boy, a face that looked unmistakably angry.

The dark lad ignored Peter's efforts at freeing himself. "You, bad people. You inside *our* cave. You steal Cooracardie." He began dragging Peter into the open.

The sun struck his head and shoulders like a whiplash.

"No! Don't!" cried Anita. "Leave him alone! Listen! We're lost. . . . We don't know where we are . . . and we haven't got any more food or water. We only came in here to get out of the sun."

"You bushed?" The aboriginal boy sounded as if he had discovered the reason for their presence for himself.

"Yes, yes, we're bushed."

The boy released Peter. "You no know this land?"

"We don't," said Peter.

The aboriginal crouched into the cave and sat down. "I," he touched his bare chest, "I, Cooracardie."

The lizard had followed him and was lying close up against his legs.

Anita pointed at it. "But you said *he* was Cooracardie."

"He and me *both* Cooracardie. He is me and me is him."

"That's nonsense," said Peter. "If you . . ."

Anita nudged him. "This is *your* cave, Cooracardie?"

"Cave of my tribe. . . . You homestead people?"

Anita nodded. "From Ilara."

"You faraway from Ilara."

"We've been to Alice Springs."

"You far, far from Alice. . . . You come from smashed-up car."

"Peter, don't rush him," said Anita. "He's got to work things out."

"He's no use to us." The heat was making Peter feel irritable. "If he can't even tell us how long ago he passed our car, he won't . . ."

"Oh, be quiet!"

"He's just a silly kid."

"I tell you he knows more than we do, a lot more. It's *his* country."

"We must find out somehow. . . ."

"He'll tell us. But he's got to work it out."

Peter realized that there was nothing he could do. Anita was bound to understand the aboriginals better than he. She'd lived in Australia most of her fifteen years. She'd played with the dark kids all her life. Besides, why *shouldn't* the aboriginals do things differently? They *were* different. They didn't even look like Negroes—not any of the Negroes he'd seen in England. The skin of the aboriginals seemed almost blue tinted compared with the Negroes'; their hair was straight more than crinkled, and their features were unique—good-looking and pleasing, but not to be compared with those of any other race or nation's. Peter admitted to himself that he had never set eyes on people such as Cooracardie until he had come to the center of Australia.

Cooracardie and the lizard were sitting side by side, perfectly still. A small child, a dark boy about eight years old, had crept into the cave, and squatted down without paying attention to anyone. Cooracardie put an arm about the child's shoulders and continued to gaze into the hot bush. The three of them—child, boy, and lizard—appeared to have forgotten the strangers in their cave.

The world beyond their shelter was steeped in dazzling light. At times it looked as if the tough, gray swirls of mulga grass were turning into metal, as if the shimmering trunks of the ghost gums were about to burst into white smoke. The strange tidal patterns of red sand and the flame-red rocks—some shaped like animals or even human faces—made Peter feel lonely. This was no country for people. It was more like the landscapes of the moon, a land of frightful unfamiliarities, a place where one could die of thirst and turn to sand or stone without anyone noticing the transformation. Here the sunshine no longer meant "a fine day." Here even the sun was menacing, an element as dangerous as fire.

A sudden movement among the ghost gums made Peter's heart jump. The long, fingerlike leaves rustled. A Land Rover? Someone searching for him and Anita? A flock of rose-colored parakeets rose screeching to the sky, their white crests glinting like coronets. They soared up the side of a red cliff and disappeared. And the country sank back into its inhuman desert silence.

"Let's go, Anita."

She glanced at the still figures of Cooracardie, the lizard, and the child. "Wait."

"What for? We're not getting anywhere just sitting here. . . ."

"*They* are our only chance of getting rescued. Don't you understand? We're in trouble . . . real trouble. If we walked off into the bush again we'd be dead inside a day."

"How can *he* help us?"

"That's what he's trying to work out."

"What? Just squatting there?"

"He's dreaming."

"A lot of good that'll do us."

"Listen, Peter . . . he's not just sort of mooning. He's gone into dreamtime. It's something only aboriginals can do. Do you ever dream?"

"Well . . . sometimes."

"Have you dreamed of something that really happened—or of something you expected to happen?"

"There's one dream I remember . . . the night before we left London. You know, about going to Australia."

"What was it like?"

"Oh—I dreamed I was in Trafalgar Square feeding the pigeons. Then the fountain sort of turned into an ocean, and I was on a ship. Your father and mine were talking together . . . and my headmaster was there . . . and he kept asking me why I hadn't told him that your dad and mine are brothers. He said I was in trouble."

"That's it, Peter! That's a bit like Cooracardie's kind of dreaming—only not so useful. You see, in your dream everything was jumbled together. You'd *been* in Trafalgar Square and you'd *been* in trouble at school, but you were *going* to Australia, and your father and mine were *going* to talk together. At the same time you were there in your own bed. See? Things in the past and in the future were mixed together at a moment which was in the present."

"It was just a dream."

"Of course. But you saw things which you *couldn't* have seen all at the same time when you're awake. It's just what Cooracardie's doing now. Only he isn't asleep. His mind is doing . . . well, a walkabout in days that have passed and in days that haven't yet happened."

"Would he know that he's *here, now?*"

"I think so. It's the aboriginal's way of working out problems. Anything to do with the bush—past, present, and sometimes future—they sort of see and smell things. We wouldn't even know that they exist. It's a special magic."

"Magic! Silly!"

"Wait and see, Peter."

"What would your father say if he heard you talk such nonsense?"

"Father?" Anita smiled. "It's he who told me. He explained to me that the aboriginals—not so much the few who work on our homestead—are nomadic people. They wander about the bush. They don't grow food, and yet they survive in a country which is mostly desert most of the year. What do you think would happen to them if they didn't have some sort of special knowledge? How would they find enough to eat and drink . . . and shelter? Do you know what size the Northern Territory is? It's as big as France and Germany put together. And that's only a part of the aboriginal lands. Do you know the size of our farm?"

"Yes, I know it's big."

"Six hundred square miles. Just the one farm. Peter, we'd get lost on our own homestead if we didn't have our aboriginal trackers, and cattlemen like Minu. Now do you see what I mean? About Cooracardie being our only hope of getting out of here?"

"I hope Cooracardie *is* dreaming and not just asleep."

A shadow passed across Peter's vision. Something squawked. The child stretched out an arm, and a little parakeet alighted on his index finger. It stretched its grass-green wings, flicked the scarlet tail, and then contentedly went to sleep, beak tucked into the downy feathers beneath its quills.

Cooracardie grinned. "My brother, Tabalu—he special say with all animal. . . . Man no more with smashed-up car. Man gone. *You* say."

"He's saying that your father's been rescued," Anita told Peter. "He wants to know how it happened."

Cooracardie nodded.

"Peter's father, that's my uncle, Peter, and I went to pick

up the mail in Alice Springs," explained Anita. "We did some shopping, and it got rather late. We didn't want to spend the night in Alice, because we'd have had to leave at dawn in any case. My dad had told us not to drive in the heat. So, Uncle John kept going all night. He'd served in the Western Desert in the war, so the bush didn't worry him. He did all right."

"You no get stuck in bull dust?"

"Oh, once or twice, but we had mats and a spade with us. Then we came to that creek."

"It looked the same as all the other creeks we'd crossed," said Peter.

"The ground had a different feel," Anita reminded him. "But the banks weren't steep, so Uncle John went into bottom gear and drove down. Next thing, everything sort of broke up. We plunged down through layers and layers of sand . . . and the car kept rocking from side to side, and then it turned right over. We were all right—Peter and I—but Uncle John got knocked out. We couldn't *see* any injuries, but I think he broke some ribs. . . . Our compass was smashed too. . . ."

Cooracardie frowned. "So you go walk."

"Yes," said Anita, in a small voice. "I knew about not walking off when you've had a breakdown . . . but, you see, I thought I recognized the rocks. We wanted to get help fast because of Uncle John. . . . It's lucky our people found him so soon. If they hadn't . . ."

"*Your* people no find." Cooracardie grinned. "Is *my* people take sick man away."

"Oh no!" Peter felt scared. This was as bad as the moment when he'd first realized that his father had become totally helpless. "He was hurt. . . . Anita, if they were rough with him . . . What will they do with Father?"

"He'll be looked after. . . . Cooracardie, how do you know *who* found Uncle John? Didn't they wear shoes?"

"*One*' with shoes. But I know my people walk like no white man." There was pride in the boy's uptilted face. "I know aboriginals go help sick man. I know is people of Kukatja. I know is people with good medicine man."

"*How* do you know?" asked Peter, suspiciously.

Cooracardie regarded him, laughter in his eyes. "*Altjira* tell me."

"Dreamtime," said Anita.

"I know more," Cooracardie assured them. "Kukatja take away sick man two days one night past."

Cooracardie took over, and it seemed right. His tribe, he explained, was camped three days' distant, in a place he knew between the cave and Ilara farm. Peter and Anita were to walk home with him and Tabalu. Then a man of his tribe would take a message to Ilara.

Peter realized that it would be a week before Anita's parents would know that they were alive—a whole week before *he'd* know how his father was. But he could think of no better plan. At least he believed that his father was not lying dead in this awful heat.

His own throat had begun to feel as if someone had stuffed it with grit. His throat was hurting. "Got any water?" he asked Cooracardie. He noticed the damp patches on Anita's shirt, the beads of moisture on his own forehead. And suddenly he felt shy of Cooracardie and little Tabalu with their cool, velvet-dark faces and those large, calm eyes.

"Water, no," said Cooracardie, apologetically. He took a cotton-covered bundle off his belt, and untied the knots. "This, better." He gave Peter a thick, silvery leaf. "Eat . . .

is good." He handed another to Anita. "Good?"

The stuff tasted like some pungent medicine. It reminded Peter of the ointment the schoolmatron had rubbed on his chest to cure his bronchitis. He was tempted to spit out the leaf, but Cooracardie's watchfulness made him swallow. Within moments a wonderful coolness spread from his stomach to his throat, and his mouth felt as if he'd been drinking iced water.

"Yes," he said, "it's good."

Cooracardie smiled. "Now we go, make food."

He led the way out of the cave, the lizard dangling from his shoulder. Tabalu, who still hadn't spoken, followed with the little parakeet asleep on his head.

They scrambled down a crumbling rock face, edged along a shelf in the side of a serrated hill and suddenly found themselves on a plateau. The west side of this natural terrace overlooked the vast valleys of sand and ghost gums, the gigantic rocks which were turning from daytime flame red to evening purple. At the back of the terrace the stones, already drained of color, were honeycombed with caverns and fissures.

Cooracardie gave a sharp whistle, and presently a dog came trotting out of the rocks. He was a lean, tawny animal with suspicious eyes and alert, pointed ears.

"Tabalu." Cooracardie spoke to the small boy in a language Peter couldn't understand.

The child went to the dog, put a hand on its head, and together they disappeared through a gap in the stones.

"It's a wild dog," whispered Anita.

"Dingo," agreed Cooracardie. "Dingo much angry. But Tabalu, he special say with all animal." He went scrabbling inside a hole covered with loose stones. "I tell Tabalu go walk, so he no see . . . so he no cry." He held up a couple of dead rabbits. "Tabalu, he come back when we done cooking."

Peter wiped his mouth with the back of his hand and leaned against the rocks. He thought he'd never eaten better roast meat. The charcoal, made of eucalyptus wood, had given the rabbits a flavor at once spicy and fragrant. There had been more than sufficient for them all, including the dingo dog.

The evening was very clear—as if the myriad particles of red dust had wearied of their dance in the sun and floated to rest. The darkness was not really dark; above the man-shaped silhouettes of rocks and the deeper shadows of sand valleys, the sky covered the bush like a lid made of engraved silver.

The patterns of single stars and constellations shone with the brightness of small flames. And the stars seemed almost within touching distance—they looked so large. Peter, re-membering his father's remark that he was near the Tropic of Capricorn, had a strange feeling that his geography master had omitted telling him the real meaning of Capri-corn—that the sky along that geographical line sagged with its weight of stars, until it came close to touching the mountains of the planet Earth.

"Peter, you aren't listening," said Anita.

"I heard."

Cooracardie had been telling them about the mission of Hermannsburg where he and Tabalu were "made educated" until they ran away. Cooracardie might have been speaking of an English boarding school. His parents had left the two boys at the mission with instructions to work well, to learn English and the skills of the white man. New ways were spreading throughout the bush; the ancestral life of the aboriginals was slowly changing. Because the white man was turning ever greater tracts of bush into farming lands, the aboriginal tribes were finding ever less to hunt and eat. The country which had sustained the lives of many tribes was shrinking year by year. Soon there would be no tribes of the old school—only aboriginals attached to homesteads, strangers in their own country, working alongside the white man. Unless . . . Perhaps if the aboriginals learned the skills of the white man . . . Perhaps if aboriginals and Australians became partners of the deserts . . . Cooracardie's parents had wanted their boys to fit themselves for a new way of living—a way that they still found sad and bewildering.

Tabalu had been happy at Hermannsburg. In the hundred-odd square miles of the mission he had found many animals to play with and to love. The food had been good, the teachers kindly. Cooracardie too had become fond of the people who had taught him and taken care of him— especially of old Pastor Jonathan. But Cooracardie had been older than Tabalu when they'd arrived at Hermannsburg —almost thirteen. And throughout his years at the mission, he had been unable to forget.

He could not forget the excitement of reading the language of the sand, the faint marks that proclaimed the presence of a quarry. He could not forget the thrill of watching a spear arc through the air and strike down the kangaroo the family would eat for supper around the campfire. The mission's tame steak and kidney pie would remind Cooracardie of kangaroo roasted on eucalyptus charcoal, the singing in church of his own people's drums and the deep trumpet note of the songman's *didjeridu*. The mission singing had sounded all right, but it hadn't been as good as *his* people's corroborees, when family and friends had sung of their hunting and of the white man's works—when the fun and the laughter had taken all pain and fear and anger out of their hearts.

But most of all, Cooracardie had remembered the old men of his tribe—the leaders who had governed with dignity and authority and who had taught him to understand the languages of sand and rocks, of birds, animals, trees, sun, and stars.

Neither the patience and affection of his teachers nor his long talks with Pastor Jonathan had made Cooracardie forget that other way of living. Nor had he ever lost the feeling that his stay at the mission was unimportant, that his real life would begin with his return to his own Maka Aranda tribe.

One day *altjira*, the eternal dreamtime, had told him that one of his people was sick. And a few days later, Pastor Jonathan had said that his mother was in the hospital in Alice Springs. She was not "very sick" though. But Cooracardie knew better. He had to help his mother. *Altjira* was calling him home.

Cooracardie and Peter looked at one another across the flickering embers of their fire. The aboriginal boy's arms were entwined with the lizard, one hand stroking the curled tail.

"What can you do?" asked Peter. "How can going back to your tribe help your mother?"

"I must see medicine man."

"She'll be getting good medicine at the hospital," said Anita.

Cooracardie shook his head. "They no know about bad magic. Our medicine man make her right because he take away the bad magic."

Magic! In London Peter would have laughed out loud. But on a night like this it didn't seem so impossible. The fierce white moonlight had changed the bush yet again. The rocks were clearly visible, yet they were no color one could name, nor was their substance recognizable. Those weird shapes could have been anything—paper cutouts, toy balloons, prowling animals, or the bones of men who had died thousands of years ago. And the burnished-silver trunks of the ghost gums looked like sentries, men in armor who had grown crooked and old guarding this ancient land.

Peter ducked into the low cave and stretched out beside his cousin. "Anita, do you know anything about this . . . bad magic that's supposed to make people sick?"

"Well—the aboriginals don't believe in things like germs or infection. They think it's a sort of evil spell that makes a person ill. So they ask their medicine man to undo the curse. And it often works."

"I expect our modern drugs make it work."

"It isn't so simple. I've heard our doctor talk about it. Sometimes the hospital gets an aboriginal who's very ill, but the doctors can't find anything wrong with him. And drugs don't help at all. Often such patients just die—sort of without a reason. But if relatives visit someone like that and tell him that the medicine man has taken away the bad magic, he recovers."

"It's rubbish, isn't it?"

"I don't know, Peter. After all *our* people pray for the sick. We think it helps."

"That's different."

"Is it though?"

"Maybe it isn't different for *them*," admitted Peter.

He was watching the two boys beside the fire, still thinking about the aboriginals and their magic, when he suddenly saw Cooracardie lean forward and put his hand into the red-hot embers.

Anita gasped as if *she* had been burned.

"He must be crazy!" Peter was waiting for Cooracardie to snatch his hand out of the fire. But the aboriginal boy was sitting unmoved, apparently unaware of any kind of pain. "He couldn't be *asleep?*"

"No, he isn't asleep. . . . I think he must be training. So *that's* why he's run away from the mission."

"He told us why."

"He told us only part of the story, Peter. I expect his mother *is* sick. But what really made him return to the bush is . . . he believes it's time for him to be grownup. He must be about our age—fifteen or sixteen. You see, the aboriginals have special ceremonies . . . something to do with making boys grownup by giving them secret knowledge, and also by making them stand up to pain to test their courage."

"Look!"

Cooracardie had quietly withdrawn his hand from the fire. He lay down, and instantly fell asleep.

Peter shook his head. "His hand must be in a mess. And he doesn't seem to care."

"I don't think you'll see any burns in the morning. This is something only aboriginals can do."

"I once saw a man eat fire—in a circus."

"Suppose some whites can train themselves too."

"It's crazy, all the same."

"Cooracardie's only trying to be ready for his initiation ceremonies."

"They're certainly heathens, these people."

"Don't know. Christian churches have confirmation. . . . It's a similar idea. You know, being grownup enough to pledge yourself . . . well, to live like an adult Christian."

"We have a Jewish boy at school. He told us he was getting instruction for bar mitzvah. And when he knows the right prayers and all that, his people hold a ceremony for him. And afterward, he's recognized as a grownup."

"Yes, I think that's how the aboriginals see it. Maybe it's even more important to them. My father says the secret ceremonies are bound up with knowledge of how to survive in the bush. That's as far as any of us know."

"These people needn't live like savages. They could work on homesteads, like Minu."

"They don't want to—most of them. Even Minu disappears sometimes. He goes walkabout and we never know whether he's coming back, or where he's been."

Anita's voice seemed to come from a great distance. Peter's eyes closed. Then he began to dream; he was running through meadows, chasing after his grandmother's beagles. The dogs were leaping through the long grass, whinnying and barking, pursuing some kind of lizard.

Suddenly he heard a scream. He shot up and hit his head on the roof of the cave. No, the yelling hadn't been a dream. Nor the yelping. Under the gun-metal gray sky, a pack of ugly yellow dogs had surrounded Cooracardie. Peter saw their bared fangs, the hungry glitter of their eyes. One of the brutes was tearing at Cooracardie's trousers.

"Tabalu! Tabalu!"

The little boy came out of his cave, sleepily rubbing his eyes. His dog, following him, stiffened, gave a strange whine, and suddenly plunged into the hostile pack.

Tabalu gave some command which brought the dog back

to his side, apparently unhurt. Then, together, they advanced on the howling pack. They walked with slow, step-by-step deliberation, Tabalu talking softly in his incomprehensible language.

Boy and dog somehow penetrated into the middle of the pack without drawing the attackers upon them. The dingos were still snatching at Cooracardie's flailing arms and legs. Tabalu went on talking. Gradually he began touching their bodies, gently pushing aside the most aggressive of the animals.

The howling and yelping ceased. The dingoes hung their heads, pawed the ground, and even wagged tails. They now looked like animals who had no idea what there was to be excited about.

Tabalu, speaking to the biggest dingo, put his hand on his back and walked with him toward the steep path which led to the sands below. The dog seemed to accompany him willingly, and the pack followed.

At the head of the path Tabalu stopped, and whispered in the animal's ear. For a moment the dingo and he looked at one another. Then the big tawny creature stepped on to the path, and quietly led his pack down between the rocks.

Cooracardie turned to Peter and Anita. "Is good. Tabalu, he special say with all animal."

If Cooracardie had been afraid of those ferocious wild dogs, he now showed no sign of it. "Is good. We walk now or sun will make much hot air."

Early though it was, the flies were awake. As Peter began to eat what was left of his supper, the flies arrived in thick, black swarms, settling greedily on the scraps of rabbit, on Peter's nostrils, eyes, and lips. They did not bite, but the tickling and crawling were no less irritating.

He put aside a half-eaten leg of rabbit.

Anita looked up, and laughed. "If you're worried about germs—well, you needn't be. These flies don't carry infection. They're not like city flies that feed on refuse, because there aren't any cities for thousands of miles."

"Flies belong here," said Cooracardie. "They make no bad."

"Oh . . ." Peter bit into the meat, but not without first blowing off the flies. "They're just a nuisance."

The sun was still invisible, nothing more than a warmth on one's face, when they began the day's march.

After Anita had sunk up to her waist into a pool of the fine bull dust, they took to walking in single file behind Cooracardie. At times Peter was tempted to ask the aboriginal boy why he was taking a wide curve around a single column of rock or avoiding a stretch of mulga grass. But so purposefully did Cooracardie make his way that questions became impossible; they would have sounded mistrustful—or worse, childish.

Toward midday Peter saw an obviously man-made pile of boulders. The shade of the ghost gums made it an ideal resting place. But Cooracardie ignored the grove, and walked on.

The furnace heat of the sun made Peter feel sick with tiredness and thirst. "What's the point of going on?" he asked irritably. "Let's stop here."

"No good," said Cooracardie, without turning around. "Spirit here bad for Maka Aranda people. We, fire people. This place of rainbow snake."

"All right, but what about the creek over there?" Peter pointed to the gully, whose steep right bank provided a strip of shade. "It'll do."

"No . . . *kardaitchas* live here . . . spirit men."

"Not *more* evil spirits! Anita, can you smell anything to be scared about?"

"I'm tired." Anita flopped down. "I don't care if we meet the devil himself as long as we get out of this sun."

Cooracardie looked at them. "Yes . . . is killer sun." He gazed at the great reaches of sand, the flame-red boulders, the blinding light. Then, without a word, he pulled Anita to her feet, and led his party into the dry, narrow river bed.

They huddled in the shade, and shared the leaves Cooracardie had collected. This time the pungent flavor of the plants did not refresh Peter so well. The heat seemed to press down upon him with the whole weight of the sky. Even his drowsiness was no relief. Nor did it help that Cooracardie looked restless and worried.

The last thing Peter saw before he fell asleep was Cooracardie stooped over a patch of gravel, his forehead puckered in an unhappy frown. He was speaking to Tabalu, pointing to something on the ground.

The thing that jerked him awake was nothing more than a slight movement of the hot air—something less than a breeze. Opening his eyes with an effort, he discovered that Anita and the two boys were intently watching a point south of the creek.

"Will it come our way?" asked Anita.

"Maybe yes, maybe no." Cooracardie shaded his eyes. "He always dance here and there."

Suddenly Peter saw it—a tall pink object shaped like a pillar. And it *was* dancing—leaping about the bush like a mad circus clown on stilts. It was hopping toward them with fantastic speed, becoming taller and wilder in its erratic progress—and somehow more terrifying.

"What is it?" Sand blew into Peter's mouth, and made him cough.

"It's called a willy-willy," said Anita. "It's a localized sandstorm. You get lots of them in the bush."

The calm statement didn't make the thing more reassuring. As the willy-willy came leaping nearer, Peter saw that the crazy dancer consisted of sand. Each particle seemed to revolve and tumble about within the orbit of the giant pillar.

"Down!" shouted Cooracardie.

The sky went dark, and all at once Peter felt as if a swarm of bees had descended on him. The sand, hitting every exposed bit of skin, hurt like a thousand stings. His ears, his mouth, and nostrils filled with grit. It seemed hours before he could take a breath without choking.

"Ooh!" Anita sat up, shaking her hair. It had changed from blond to pink. "That was lucky!"

"Lucky?" Peter touched the tender spots on his arms.

"And how! You don't know. The main part of it missed us. If that willy-willy had gone right over us it would have knocked us out—or worse. Do you realize? A willy-willy that size can overturn a Land Rover."

The pillar was still dancing, leaping ahead on the other side of the creek, zigzagging from side to side. Now it looked like a sprite, a gamboling ghost, a delinquent creature delighting in mischief.

"Bad spirits." Cooracardie, still flat on his stomach, put his ear to the ground. "We go?"

"It's still too hot for walking," objected Anita.

"*Kardaitchas*, they angry." Cooracardie continued his examination of the ground. "Sand here say big animal fight . . . animal wild angry."

"Oh! Stop worrying!"

Cooracardie sat back on his haunches. Anita and Peter grinned at one another; Cooracardie was quite funny when he showed silent disapproval. Yet the others too showed signs of uneasiness. The lizard, Cooracardie, had stuck its head into the Spinifex grass, pretending to be part of the clump, and the dingo dog—halfway up the steep bank—was prowling to and fro, nose aquiver, upright ears twitching with nervousness.

The dingo had begun to whine.

"We go?" asked Cooracardie.

"All right," Anita agreed.

Cooracardie began to climb the steep bank on the north side of the creek, making for Tabalu who was busy pacifying his dog.

Peter, about to cross the river bed, heard a peculiar new sound—somewhat like steam escaping through a valve. He noticed a puff of sand splattering toward him along the creek.

Suddenly he was down. Black spots flickered in front of

his eyes, and he appeared to be bumping over a rutted field. It was like the time he had collided with Wilson at the beginning of a soccer match at school.

The sounds above him, a kind of pounding and trumpeting, made him curl up and tuck his head under his arms. He remembered, almost with leisure, that Anita had shouted to him. And he remembered Cooracardie's talk of big animals fighting.

"Peter!" shouted Anita. "Come on! Don't just lie there! Come up! Quick!"

He managed to pick himself up and crawl to the bank. "Hurry!"

Still bent double, he began to scramble up. Anita grabbed him.

"What . . ." he began.

Anita pointed into the river bed. "Keep still!"

The animal stood almost touching the steep banks on either side. It was an enormous camel. Facing Tabalu and Cooracardie, it had bared its vicious-looking yellow teeth and was emitting unpleasant, snarling sounds. The creature was angry, and it looked so dangerous that Peter expected it to charge the two aboriginals. But the boys stood their ground, and Tabalu was talking—talking in the strange language of the Aranda. It was as musical as poetry.

"*Anbalu radi maka takaaba andama . . . anbalu radi . . .*"

The camel lifted its head and stared down its nose, not unlike an elderly bachelor schoolmaster demanding some proof of *school spirit*.

Tabalu, continuing his incomprehensible lecture, pointed to the ground.

The camel flicked its eyelids, turning its head as if the words had an offensive smell.

Tabalu, talking all the time, stepped forward, still pointing to the ground.

The camel snorted unpleasantly, but it did not rush the little boy. It even began to look uncertain.

"*Anbalu!*"

Suddenly the camel's front legs buckled. It sank to its knees and the long neck stretched until its head touched the sand.

Now Tabalu advanced with confidence. His small hands began to scratch the animal behind the ears, much as he'd caress his dingo. The big camel looked perfectly peaceful. Tabalu called Cooracardie. They bent over the camel together, apparently examining a spot on its cheek.

Cooracardie searched his pockets. He produced some leaves which he put on the camel's face, and then he tied up the dressing with a blue handkerchief. The camel, looking somewhat sulky but none the less more like a domestic pet than a wild creature, watched the boys climb the bank. For dignity's sake it hesitated, but when the boys reached the top it began to follow them.

"He angry bull camel. He make big fight. Other bull camel bite his face," explained Cooracardie. "Now Tabulu make safe. You ride?"

Neither Peter nor Anita felt trustful enough. Once out of the creek they were prepared to walk again. Only Tabalu was confident enough to make the camel kneel again and to mount him.

"Where did he come from?" asked Peter.

"He's one of the wild ones," Anita told him.

"Didn't know you had camels in this country. It looks . . . all wrong."

"I know what you mean. Actually there weren't any camels in Australia until the last century. The explorers who discovered the Northern Territory used horses to begin with. But the bush was too tough on them for long journeys. Too many died of thirst and heat. So the early settlers imported camels and drivers from Asia. . . . The train from the south to Alice Springs is still called the Ghan, after the first Afghan camel caravans."

"Now the camels are just running wild?"

"Only some. Most of them are still used for transporting goods. The aboriginals take care of them. The tribes own quite a few. But you must remember how big this country is. Some camels just drift off into the bush. They can become so wild that no man can get near them. Except Tabalu." Anita smiled. "He special say with all animal."

Tabalu, the little parakeet perched on his head, looked serene and safe astride the camel's neck; the dog behind him crouched awkwardly and seemed in danger of falling off. As for the lizard, it had selected to remain on Cooracardie's shoulder.

"Shaab . . . Shaab," said Tabalu, grinning down from his impressive height.

"Name of camel," Cooracardie announced, proudly. "Tabalu, he know camel named Shaab."

In the late afternoon, the stillness of the bush was broken by a whirring and spluttering. It seemed to come toward them across the bright-blue sky. Peter half expected to see one of those great eagles he had observed hovering about the rocks before sundown. But the noise changed to a consistent throb.

"A plane!" he shouted.

They stopped, waving their arms, jumping about, shouting. The dingo barked and Shaab snorted. As if in answer, the small aircraft lost height and began to circle overhead.

Anita was the first to stop the antics. "It's probably a flying-doctor plane. A single-engined Cessna," she added, flatly.

"It must be for us!" shouted Peter. "Don't just stand there! They're searching for us! See the pilot? Look!"

"Don't. You're just making yourself hot and tired," said Anita, gently.

"They'd have seen us, if . . ."

"If what?"

Yes, what? Peter looked at himself, at his companions and the animals. His light jeans and shirt had changed color like Anita's. Probably even his hair had gone as pink as hers. And the darkness of Tabalu and Cooracardie was the darkness of the rock caves, their trousers the color of the Spinifex grass.

It was as if all of them, including the tawny dingo and the dun camel, had become a part of the bush, indistinguishable from sand and rock. Even the parakeet's tail feathers were but another shade of desert red; even they disappeared against the sun and the flame-colored sand. How small they were, all of them—so much smaller than such landmarks as ghost gums and dried-up river beds.

The aboriginal boys, in the baggy trousers that were much too big for them, might have looked like kangaroos from that plane—that is if the pilot had seen anything at all apart from bush and more bush. Perhaps if the camel had kept walking . . . But its movement wouldn't have been noticed from a plane in much faster motion.

No, their party was totally insignificant in this vastness, as insignificant as the endless swarms of flies.

"Don't be miserable." Anita put her hand on Peter's shoulder. "Cooracardie's people will help us. It's only one more day. Tomorrow we'll make the camp."

The camel lifted its nose, and stopped. Shaab's naturally disapproving face assumed an air of furious stubbornness.

With his injured cheek still tied up in the blue handkerchief, he looked more than ever like an outraged disciplinarian. His nostrils quivered. He snorted, and wouldn't move on.

"Camp," said Cooracardie.

What Peter saw was a curious citadel of red towers some fifteen or twenty feet high, which might have been the remains of ruined Norman castles if the Normans had ever got to the Northern Territory. Strange homes, even as temporary ones for aboriginals. Then he remembered. These sand towers were the work of termite ants—the only builders in this emptiness.

"Camp." Cooracardie pointed into the distance.

At last Peter could make out the signs of habitation. He knew he would not have discovered them by himself—neither the gossamer haze in the sky which was the only mark of campfires, nor the outline of the broken, red-stone walls.

A mile or so farther on he saw that the walls—possibly the remains of an old farm—had been reconstructed into some kind of shelters. A hut, made of corrugated iron, had turned as red as the stones, and even the scattered petrol-drums blended into the flame-colored landscape.

Cooracardie turned his party away, east of the camp. He stopped at a long, flat-topped rock honeycombed with caves.

"We go, say about you." He sounded uneasy. "You stay here."

"Just Peter and me?" asked Anita.

"Yes."

"Couldn't we all . . ."

"No." Cooracardie looked intently at the pattern he was drawing in the sand with his bare toes. "I speak with father of my father. Say, you here, you bushed. *He* say about *you*."

"How long . . . ?"

"We go," said Cooracardie firmly.

The odd little caravan turned back toward the camp. Within minutes it had disappeared among the hot sand dunes and the red rocks.

"I can't really understand it," admitted Anita. "Usually the aboriginals are kind. They'd share anything with you—shelter, food, water—especially in the bush. I've never known a mean aboriginal."

"Cooracardie didn't look happy about leaving us here," said Peter. "Maybe we should have refused to . . ."

"No, that would have been . . . like making someone put you up for the weekend, someone who doesn't want you around."

"He didn't even say anything about sending a messenger to Ilara."

"I know." Anita sat down on the stone slab outside the cave Cooracardie had allotted them. "But he won't forget," she said without much conviction.

"We could just walk into their camp."

"Not really, Peter."

"You make it sound like gate crashing the Governor General's tea party."

"It would be just as rude."

"Nuts."

"Look, all you've met are our aboriginal trackers and cattlemen . . . and a couple of aboriginal kids. But that doesn't mean you know anything about these people. Even those of us who live here find them pretty mysterious."

"You've *told* me how marvelous the aboriginals are, so you needn't start on that line again."

"They *are* marvelous, Peter. When it comes to living in

the bush among their own people, they're more civilized than we are. They treat one another politely. They share all their possessions with their families and the tribe. They don't kill—except when they go hunting food. They . . ."

"They believe in ghosts. . . ."

"Spirits. So what! Some white people do. At least *their* spirits make sense. The way they look at it, animals, plants, rocks, sand, the sky . . . everything is part of a complete universe. They believe that all things of the universe are . . . well, a part of the spirit of creation. Why not? Don't we believe in a Maker . . . God?"

"That's different."

"The vicar doesn't think so."

"Which?"

"The vicar of Alice Springs."

"Then he's a heathen."

"Oh!" Anita turned, abruptly. "*You'll* grow up one of these days. . . . Peter! Look!" Anita, pointing toward the dunes behind which Cooracardie had vanished, seemed to have forgotten her anger. "Look! They're coming."

They were an old woman and a girl about Anita's age— and the lizard Cooracardie.

The lizard lay down between Peter and Anita as trustfully as if they'd never tried to trap it. The old woman put down a tin can of liquid, something which looked like doughy bread, and a platter made of interwoven leaves containing barbecued meat.

The granny and the girl smiled, indicated that Peter and Anita were to eat, and made to go.

"Oh, please!" called Anita.

"We want to come with you." Peter seized the girl by the sleeve of her cotton blouse.

The girl shook her head.

"Tell us at least whether your people have sent off someone with a message," pleaded Anita.

The granny patted Anita's cheek.

"Peter, they don't know English. . . . Ilara . . . Ilara . . ." Anita repeated the name of her homestead "Ilara!"

Clearly the name meant nothing to the two aboriginals.

"Let them go," said Anita.

"But we must find out. . . ."

"It's no use."

"Are we supposed to stay here all night?"

"Looks like it." Anita stroked the lizard's back. "Cooracardie sent his familiar anyway."

"His what?"

"His familiar. Don't you remember? He said *he* was the lizard and the lizard was *him*. It's . . . well, they sort of belong together. Sending us his lizard is Cooracardie's way of being with us."

"It would have been less complicated if Cooracardie himself had turned up and told us what's happening."

"Maybe not. Look, we just don't know about this tribe."

"We only know they're marvelous," Peter baited her.

Anita didn't answer. She picked up a piece of bread and began to eat.

As the lilac and purple colors of dusk faded to darkness, strange, tapping sounds drifted from the aboriginals' camp, softly at first, then with the fullness of drums.

Peter could not see Anita's face, but he had a feeling that even she was scared. Everything about the night was weird —the wild beat of instruments which sounded like drums and yet didn't, the stagnant heat of the low-roofed cave, the peculiar nearness of the stars, and, not least, the impression that men—under cover of rocks and ghost gums —were creeping close.

Suddenly Anita cried out.

"Animals!"

Peter groped about the dark. Something pushed against him, something warm and furry. Then it was brushing his hand, and the touch seemed familiar. "Dingo!"

A yap, which sounded excited but friendly.

"Oh, Tabalu's dog!" Anita giggled with relief. "Suppose he's been sent to look after us."

"I'd rather have people looking after us. . . . What's this?" A loud trumpeting had risen above the drumbeats. The note quavered in the still air, appearing to hang there unable to drop. "What is it?"

"I think I know now. The aboriginals must be having some ceremony. The beat must be boomerangs they're tapping together. The trumpet thing is a *didjeridu* . . . a hollow piece of wood, about four feet long, with a mouthpiece made of hardened gum."

"You've heard this kind of . . . music before?"

"Yes, at corroborees. They're song and dance feasts."

"They let you watch?"

"Of course. I've been to lots of corroborees."

"Then why can't we go to this one?"

"Peter, I don't know. Somehow it's different. It doesn't sound quite the same as the other corroborees. Oh . . . go to sleep."

Crawling well into the cave, they found that the floor had been covered with clean, scented mulga. The whisper of the dry grass told them that the lizard and the dingo were making their beds between them. If Cooracardie and Tabalu had sent the animals to comfort them, they'd succeeded. For the first time since their arrival, both Peter and Anita felt that *someone* was making them welcome.

But in the middle of the night Peter wakened. The

darkness was full of noises, all totally unfamiliar. The "drums" sounded faster and louder. And there were new sounds—shrill screams followed by a wailing that might have been produced by animals or women.

The luminous sunlight of the morning made Peter wonder whether he hadn't dreamed those frightening sounds. The bush looked golden and safe; the dingo was stretching all fours, yawning happily; the lizard Cooracardie was hunting its breakfast of flies, and Shaab—in the near distance—was standing majestically still, admiring his humpy shadow.

"What shall we do today?" asked Peter.

Anita smiled, instantly aware that her cousin had at last made up his mind to accept her superior knowledge of the bush. "I expect you'd still like to go to the camp."

"Maybe we could look around without being seen."

"Suppose we could . . . as long as we're here when they bring our food."

"We're not prisoners, are we?"

"Not exactly." Anita sat staring ahead. "Midday would be best. They might be asleep then. It'll be awfully hot though."

"I don't mind. Come on, we haven't yet seen *this* mountain."

They climbed to the flat top from where they could make out the stone shelters of the camp, a nearby clump of big water gum trees, and a canyon in the red rocks that looked like a concealed water hole. Peter reckoned there'd be sufficient cover for watching the camp unobserved.

When they returned to their cave, their tin can had been replenished with the aromatic liquid they had drunk the night before. The can was covered with a pale loaf wrapped in leaves, and beside this meal stood a tin of water, probably meant for washing.

"They won't come back before evening," said Anita.

After "breakfast" they explored the other caves, and found some drawings of arrows and snakes. But the morning passed slowly. They were waiting for the hour of high heat. And when it came, dusty and suffocating, they left the dingo asleep in the cave, the lizard in the shadow of a stone, and descended into the burning sand.

For a mile or so they walked in silence, alert for any movement. But the only living thing they encountered was Shaab asleep under a water gum. The trees brought them in sight of the camp and afforded them fairly good cover.

At first it seemed as if the camp had been deserted. Then, gradually, they began to see shapes other than the red shelters and the clumps of mulga grass. They noticed a mound of stones and eucalyptus branches, and they became aware of a woman squatting beside it, who was rocking to and fro, lamenting in a a low murmur.

"A grave?" asked Peter.

Anita nodded. She pointed to the place they'd guessed to be a water hole.

Under the bushes of the entrance, several men were occupied in building a kind of ladder. They were tying rough branches across two upright poles. Every now and again one of the aboriginals would step on the bars as if to test his strength. After some time, the ladder was hoisted against the steep, rock face of the canyon. Apparently the men had no intention of making it high enough to reach the top.

The ladder completed and in place, one of the workers fixed a rope to the highest rung. He then grasped the loop and let his body swing freely over a drop of some thirty feet. Satisfied with the test, he climbed down. Then he squatted beside a flat rock and began to sharpen what looked like a long, thin-bladed kitchen knife.

"Let's go," whispered Anita.

They did not speak until they were back at the foot of their own mountain. Peter was trying to remember some tale of savages who were in the habit of killing and eating their prisoners. Such people existed. He'd read about them in a newspaper shortly before he'd left England.

"I don't know what they're up to," admitted Anita.

Peter started to climb the rocks toward their cave. What choice did they have? If they fled into the bush they'd never be found—not by their own people—except as bleached skeletons. If they stayed here . . . A shadow fell across his outstretched arm. *Someone* was waiting for them.

Cooracardie, the lizard at his side, watched silently until they had climbed the ledge in front of the cave. Peter and Anita could not bring themselves to ask questions. They felt ashamed of having snooped around the camp, and awkward, afraid of showing their suspicions.

"Man gone Ilara," said Cooracardie simply. "He take word, he take your people here."

"Thank you." Peter thought of the ladder, the rope, the sharpened knife. If the tribe meant to kill them, would a message have been sent to the family—saying they were alive? Or was Cooracardie lying?

The aboriginal boy looked at him with sadness. "My father's father, he dead."

"Sorry," muttered Anita.

"Bad Kukatja man kill him."

Anita shook her head, stopping Peter from speaking. "It's not what you think. . . . Cooracardie, do your people believe that someone pointed a bone at your grandfather?"

"Yes, he die because of bad magic."

"Do *you* believe that?"

"Me know nothing." Cooracardie swallowed hard, wiping a tear which was escaping down his cheek. "Me know nothing. . . . Pastor Jonathan say *no* bad magic, only good magic. Here . . ."

"I know what you mean." Anita went to sit beside him. "Now you're with your own people, Pastor Jonathan and the things they taught you at Hermannsburg Mission are— sort of far away."

Cooracardie nodded. "Pastor Jonathan, good man. He say truth. . . . My people, good people, say truth too. . . . What is *real* truth?"

"Maybe it's like my father says," said Anita. "He's told me your people have a lot of knowledge about how to run things—I mean how to live in the bush, and how to run the tribes so they don't fight or split up. We run things much the same way—only there are more of us, so everything's more complicated. We need more government."

"You make war. We no make war."

"We try not to have wars."

"Our dreamtime teach no make war."

"Christianity teaches the same. Our religion isn't so different from yours. At least, my father thinks the important ideas are the same—like not doing harm to people, not stealing. . . ."

"Me no know." Cooracardie stubbornly avoided Anita's eyes. "You say you no steal. But you *steal*. . . . Your people have cow, bull, car, house, but you keep. You no give to uncle, aunt, father's father, brother, sister, cousin. . . . So *you* steal."

"We share too. But we do it in a different way, Cooracardie."

"You no give away three part of meat-animal."

"No, but . . ."

"You no *give*. I no know. Pastor Jonathan speak like you. Pastor Jonathan good man." At last Cooracardie lifted his troubled eyes. "Pastor Jonathan say *this*, my people say *that*. I go home because I need know. Now father's father dead. New headman, Loritja, he different."

"Are we going to see Loritja?" asked Peter.

"He much work."

"We don't like it here, alone."

The aboriginal boy put the lizard beside Peter. "You have Cooracardie. . . . You have dingo."

"They aren't people. Why can't we be in your camp? If you'd come to us, we wouldn't put you in a cave a mile from the house."

"Loritja, he much work. . . . You stay," pleaded Cooracardie.

"Well?" asked Peter, as soon as Cooracardie had left them. "*Are* we staying?"

"Maybe we could find out what they're up to." Anita watched Cooracardie run through the sand. In his baggy, oversized trousers, he looked as clumsy and as swift as a kangaroo. "I think his people *are* all right—really. I mean, I'm sure Cooracardie likes us."

"Yes. Maybe that's why he's so unhappy. Anita, do aboriginals eat—people?"

"Ours don't."

"You *know* I'm not talking about the aboriginals at Ilara."

"I don't know about the ones in the bush. You hear stories. But *I* don't believe they're cannibals."

"You don't know though, do you?"

It took them a long time to find a hiding place, dark yet close enough to the camp. The fire in front of the stone shelters lit the night so brightly that Peter and Anita were afraid to move from the strip of mulga grass behind the outcrop of rock. Even so, it seemed at times that the tall aboriginal who was in command was looking in their direction.

He was a lean old man with a mop of white hair and eyes that glittered even at a distance. The chanting he led grew louder and wilder until some of the men jumped to their feet. Not a single woman was in sight. The men circled the mound which Peter and Anita had guessed to be the grave of Cooracardie's grandfather—the dead headman.

The single-file circle shuffled round and round in ever-faster rhythm. And when the men reached running speed, they suddenly stopped and the chanting became a long-drawn wail.

"What are they doing?" whispered Peter.

"Ssh."

It looked as if the men were stabbing at their heads with sharp objects. Their gestures were uncontrolled and violent. The frenzy burned itself out; one by one the men drifted back to the fire. It was then that Peter and Anita recognized blood—slow-flowing, glistening trickles—running down their faces. The men resumed their chanting, more quietly now, accompanied by the tapping of boomerangs.

"This could go on all night," said Anita. "Go?"

"Wait."

A single figure had emerged from the shelters, a man whose body was painted with lines in the shape of a skeleton. The "ribs" and "limbs" were much paler than his skin. He approached the grave, scooped up a handful of stones, and gave what sounded like a command.

Instantly some of the men by the fire got up, returned to

the mound, and began to demolish it. Others set alight a pile of branches about a hundred feet west of the campfire. Yet another group had squatted down and was digging into the sand.

Anita hid her face in her hands. The dead headman's body was being lifted from its grave. "It's all right," murmured Peter.

Doubtfully, she looked up. Yes, it *was* all right. Cooracardie's grandfather looked no more frightening than a statue wrapped from head to toe in a sheet. And there was gentleness and dignity in the way his bearers held him aloft, carrying him to the new grave which had been prepared. He was lowered in. The men of the tribe slowly replaced the sand over him.

The headman and the painted medicine man led the procession back to the campfire.

Now Peter *wanted* them to make a noise; he wanted to get away, back to the cave. But the figures by the fire sat still and silent. Only the headman spoke.

The deep, rich voice, droning on in the strange language, sent Peter to sleep. He dreamed he was trying to cook sausages on charcoal; the chipolatas *wouldn't* get brown, but he was getting stifled in the heat of the barbecue brazier.

A loud screeching wakened him with a start. The sun was burning down, and above him a flock of parakeets was rioting into the sky.

Anita had gone.

He found her behind one of the stone shelters, much too near the camp. "This way," she whispered.

She led him toward the canyon with the hidden water hole, in the opposite direction from their camp.

"Are you crazy!" Her disappearance had so scared Peter that he felt angry with her. "What are you trying to do?

Get us caught?"

"They've carried things to the hollow on our side of the camp. We must go back the long way or we'll run into them. Don't worry. I've been watching them. We'll be all right on this side."

"What are they doing?"

"Pulling down one of the shelters. . . . It's the mats and clothes from that shelter they're putting into the hollow. The men must be asleep. It's the women who're doing the work."

"That ceremony, or whatever it is, can't be finished yet."

"I think they're performing secret rites. That's why they won't have us in the camp."

"What's so secret about a funeral? All they seem to be doing is to bury Cooracardie's grandfather . . . more than once, in their special way."

"Obviously they don't want us to know their special ways."

"Why not, if it's all harmless?"

"Maybe they think we wouldn't understand their beliefs, that we'd laugh at them. There's another thing. Once you've given away a secret, it isn't important any more."

"So, what they're doing is important to them."

"It must be. Even old white people who've lived in Australia all their lives—farmers who have aboriginal stockmen—don't know what happens at some of these ceremonies."

"What about tonight?" asked Peter.

"If they caught us . . ."

"Well, I'd rather take a chance than stay in the cave."

They were still being welcomed "home" by the boisterous dingo when their breakfast arrived. This time granny was on her own. She put down the water, "tea," and bread, gave them a rather distracted smile, and scuttled off.

Anita and Peter dozed away the burning hours. When darkness fell, they still hadn't decided whether they'd return to the camp—chiefly because they felt tired. A girl brought them the usual leaf dish of meat, and after the meal they sat outside the cave, where the air was less heat sodden.

When the stars had reached full brightness, the bush came alive with voices, first the chatter of girls, then the fuller humming of a whole community on the move. The lights of flaming torches were creeping toward their cave.

Suddenly the lights combined into a single flame—a high, flaring tongue of fire which revealed the dark figures of men and women.

"They've set light to the things in the hollow," said Anita. "The stuff they collected in the morning. . . . We can watch from here."

The crowd began to wail, and the dingo crept into the cave.

"I wonder if they're scratching open their faces again," said Peter.

"It doesn't sound like last night."

"I think they're mad."

"Oh, I don't know. You can read in the Bible about people tearing their hair when someone important dies."

"Well, it could be their way of doing that."

They listened to the sad sounds, and watched the fire sink. Gradually small groups of torches left the hollow, the dots of light flickering through the bush. But though they were widely scattered, they all seemed to be making for the camp.

"Let's go," said Peter.

By the time they arrived at the previous night's hiding place, the women had disappeared and the men were wandering toward the water hole. A fire at the entrance to the canyon lit up the ladder propped against the rock face.

Peter took Anita's hand, and led her through the maze of boulders. "Here," he pulled her behind a rock. "It'll do, but keep your head down."

The men seemed to be forming a kind of pattern again. To the accompaniment of low chanting, an old man was pushed to the ladder. As he climbed it, rung by rung, three boys of seventeen or eighteen went to stand directly below. The chanting grew louder. The boys began to sway from the waist, spreading their arms like wings. And each arm, gashed longways, was bleeding.

The old man reached the topmost rung. He turned slowly, looking down on the boys, and grasped the rope. Putting his arms through the loop, he took his feet off the ladder, suddenly swinging free above them. There was a moment of complete silence as the old man, speaking in a thin voice, hung suspended in the air. Then each of the boys answered him. When the last one had spoken, the old man's feet groped for the ladder. He managed to find a foothold, released himself from the rope, and began to climb down. His return to earth was greeted by a shout.

It was at the moment when the shouting had spread to the whole crowd that Peter felt hands clasp the back of his neck.

"No make noise," whispered Cooracardie. "I take you home. You come quick."

He darted ahead, slipping between obstacles as swiftly as his lizard, making a wide detour around the camp. He did not speak again until they reached the silence and starlight of the bush.

"Why you spy?" In the silver sheen of the night, Cooracardie's face gleamed like polished steel. "Why you do secret watch?"

"Why do you make so many secrets?" countered Peter.

"Old chief say—ceremony secret. Maybe is right, maybe, no."

"We have seen *something*," said Anita, "last night and this evening. Wouldn't it be better if you told us what it meant?"

"You see my father's father's body?"

"We saw them open the grave and bury him again."

Cooracardie shook his head. "Maybe is better I speak. . . . They take father's father out because his spirit tell them which Kukatja man kill him. Then they put father's father in new grave for making his spirit quiet. *This* night they burn possessions of father's father because deadman things no good for live people. Make quarrel, deadman things."

"Why did they scratch their heads and their faces?"

"Is because everybody very sad. . . . Father's father, he good headman. Is also because man with most bloody face makes other ceremony."

"The one we've just seen?"

"Yes. Is secret initiation rite . . . is when boy become man. Old man on ladder drop blood on blood of boys."

"That's why their arms were cut?"

"Yes. Blood of wise old man give much strongness to blood of young."

"Is *that* all?" Anita was disappointed. "My father told me the initiation rites take weeks . . . and sometimes months, because the boys have to learn such a lot before they're accepted as adults."

"Your father say truth. Blood dropping just *one* part of ceremony. Many other part, I no know. I no see until I become man. I speak overmuch. . . . I very bad."

"Telling *us* can't be so wrong, Cooracardie. We're your friends!"

"Is wrong, Anita. But I speak because you much afraid of my people. Fear is more bad than me speaking."

"We didn't go to your camp because we were scared," said Peter, "that is—not *only* because we were scared. We were curious. . . . Well, I mean, your people are so different."

Cooracardie touched his shoulder. "Is true. You half afraid, half wish-to-know."

"What will happen tomorrow?"

"Secret ceremony."

"Like tonight?"

"No."

"What sort of ceremony?"

"You stay by your cave."

"Are we prisoners then?"

"No . . . you guest of Aranda."

"If we're your guests, we should be able to go to your camp."

Cooracardie sighed. "I very bad. But I take you tomorrow. Is secret, or Loritja he very angry. Is secret . . . tomorrow Kukatja man who kill father's father he *pay* . . . he pay with life."

Peter and Anita agreed that *something* had gone wrong. But they had no way of finding out whether it was their fault that Cooracardie did not fetch them the following evening or the night after. Had Cooracardie admitted discussing the secret rites with them? Was Loritja punishing him?

The granny kept delivering their food, drink, and washing water—punctually, rather nervously, and in complete silence.

On both nights, while they waited for Cooracardie, the camp was as quiet as if it had been deserted. Peter and

Anita went as far as the water gum trees several times without seeing anyone. The only sign of life was the muffled crying of a baby.

The best part of another day passed. Then, in the late afternoon, the dingo and the lizard disappeared, and the solitude of the bush became unbearable. Peter and Anita went searching for the animals. Straying to a patch of mulga grass between their cave and the camp, they heard faint sounds of singing. They lay in the grass, ears strained, for an hour or more. The singing grew in volume until, at last, they saw a long file of men approach the camp. Some were loaded with large bundles of wood, others were carrying "meat"—trussed kangaroo—on their heads.

In the open space, in front of the shelters, the men dumped wood and meat. Women and children came running out, dogs barked, and Shaab rose on his stately legs and followed Tabalu. The whole camp was welcoming the hunters.

Only Cooracardie was missing.

They were debating whether to keep a watch on the camp or not, when Cooracardie came trotting toward them as if he knew exactly where to find them.

"What's happened?" asked Anita. "We've been worried about you."

"I go hunt," said Cooracardie, proudly. "Now we have good kangaroo for ceremony."

"For tonight?"

"Yes. Is when Kukatja who kill father's father pay with life."

Peter was not sure he wanted to see the execution. "How do you know who did it?"

"Father's father's spirit say to medicine man. He say

Kukatja point bone of deadman on him. So Kukatja, he must pay."

Peter looked at Anita. "Well?"

"We don't have to go, do we?"

"*You* go with me." Cooracardie appeared to have forgotten his objections to letting them see the rites. "You eat. I come fetch you after."

The only reason Peter and Anita could think of for Cooracardie's changed attitude was that the aboriginal boy had accepted the fact that he could not keep them away from the camp. So, he wanted to make sure that they were efficiently hidden. It was reassuring to know that Cooracardie was concerned about their safety. Even if he had *not* revealed to them so generously the meaning of the ceremonies, they would now have trusted him.

Shortly after the night had attained full starlight he came for them, accompanied by the dingo and the lizard. He still seemed relaxed, and almost happy.

He led them to the back of the camp to a stone shelter which stood apart from the rest. Fingering the solid-looking back wall, he lifted out a stone slab almost two feet square. "We go in. . . . Come."

"There's a big opening in the front," whispered Peter. "And no door."

"No man come in here."

"Are you sure?" Anita was as doubtful as Peter.

"We stay," decided Cooracardie, still in his buoyant mood. "Sit here."

The sections of front wall on either side of the entrance were large enough to screen the three of them from the open space in front of the shelters. And their "house" remained in darkness even when the flames of the campfire grew into a blaze.

The whole community was taking part in the preparations. Boys and young men fed the fire, the old man cut up the meat, girls collected the glowing charcoal, the women attended to the roasting. Loritja, the tall, white-haired headman and the medicine man—his face and body painted—walked from group to group, laughing with the women, taking an interest in the work of the men.

What impressed Peter was the orderliness of the preparations. Not even Loritja seemed to have to tell these eighty-odd people what to do, yet they were working like a well-disciplined team. Peter, after a year as school captain, appreciated the achievement of such co-operation. Cooracardie's father's father must have been a successful leader indeed. Yet the aboriginals' belief that he was killed by a man, maybe fifty miles away, pointing a bone at him still struck Peter as a piece of barbaric superstition. Unless . . . Yes, there was one possibility. . . .

"Anita, do you know anything about telepathy?"

"Not much," she admitted.

"It's—well, since I've been in Australia I've sometimes thought 'tomorrow I'll write to my mother.' Then, when I got a letter from her I could see from the date that she must have been thinking of me at the same time. You see, telepathy *may* be a scientific phenomenon. If thoughts are electrical waves which can travel distances . . . I mean, if someone really hated Cooracardie's grandfather enough to want him dead . . ."

"Yes, I see." Anita sounded pleased. "If the aboriginals believe in telepathy then there's no reason why they shouldn't carry it a stage further . . . and believe that bone pointing could kill an enemy. So, a murder trial makes sense . . . in a strange sort of way.

"A murder trial maybe. But do you want to see them kill Kukatja?"

"Kukatja," said Cooracardie. Half a dozen men and a woman had suddenly appeared from the bush. While they were being greeted by Loritja and the medicine man, the people around the fire shifted to make room for the strangers.

One of them, painted like the medicine man, walked toward their hiding place.

"No come here," Cooracardie assured them. "He look at place for paying with life."

The man, lowering his torch, moved it back and forth close to the ground, suddenly revealing a circle about three feet in diameter. It was a wreath made of fresh eucalyptus leaves interwoven with branches of some white-flowering bush. The inspection concluded, the man returned to the campfire and sat down beside Loritja.

The headman offered him the first piece of roasted meat.

Much later, when the meal was over, Loritja began to address the assembly. His guest listened, waited until he had finished, and replied at length. The conversation went on for a long time, interrupted by an occasional murmur of agreement or objection from the crowd around the fire. The only one *outside* the party was the woman the strangers had brought. She alone had not been fed, and she looked unhappy and fearful.

"Kukatja no eat," said Cooracardie.

"But you said Kukatja was a man."

Cooracardie laughed. "Kukatja is tribe . . . big tribe like us, like Aranda."

The talking had stopped. In silence one of the young

Aranda men rose. Slowly, softly, he walked to the circle of leaves and flowers. And the people began to chant.

"Is he the one . . . ?" asked Anita.

"Yes, he is man to take life."

Suddenly Loritja lifted the *didjeridu* to his lips. At the sound of the trumpet, the whole assembly sprang to their feet.

They crowded about the young man inside the circle, but at Loritja's command they squatted down. The men began to tap their boomerangs together, the women to dance— barefeet beating the ground.

Cooracardie slid to the entrance of the shelter. Peter and Anita could not see his face, but they felt his excitement.

"They'll see us," warned Peter. He pulled Cooracardie back, but a moment later the aboriginal boy was out in front again.

"He's forgotten about us," said Anita, anxiously.

The rhythm of the boomerangs had become faster. As it reached a deafening, whirling height, the leader of the Kukatja leaped into the circle, arm outstretched. He grasped the young Kukatja woman by the wrists, and pulled her in beside him.

The Aranda man, facing them, raised a knife.

"Now!" Cooracardie's shout merged with the voices of his people. "Now Kukatja pay life!"

The old Kukatja, the girl's wrists clasped in one broad fist, gave her hands to the young Aranda man with the knife. It looked as if he were handing over for slaughter a chicken or a rabbit.

The Aranda lifted his arm. As the knife came sweeping down upon the girl, Anita covered her face. But there was no sound. Unbelieving, she raised her eyes. For a second and a third time the young man performed the gesture of killing. Then, calmly, he handed the knife to the old Kukatja, gently took the girl by the arm, and led her out of the circle toward one of the shelters.

"Now life is paid," said Cooracardie happily.

"What? They *aren't* going to kill anyone?" asked Anita.

"Kill?" Cooracardie laughed. "*We* kill? You think . . . ? You no understand my people. Kukatja man who kill father's father, he give daughter to make marriage with Aranda man. So, he pay new life to Aranda. Is right now."

"But the knife?"

"Aranda man speak with knife. . . . He say he always protect Kukatja girl. She safe. She have three sons."

"How do you know?"

"He strike knife three time. . . . *Altjira*, dreamtime say to medicine man she find spirit child by water hole. Have son. She find spirit child two time more. Dreamtime say so."

The Aranda and their guests had returned to the campfire. And now it seemed to be the children's time. The older ones were leaping through the flames to shouts of encouragement. Boys of Cooracardie's age were playing with glowing embers, showing off their courage and self-control. Girls were dancing, while the little children were climbing all over their elders in happy, uncontrolled naughtiness.

"Is *arankalelama*," said Cooracardie, laughter in his voice. "Little children give bad time to father and mother."

Anita watched a tiny urchin swing from his mother's hair, unrebuked. "That must hurt! Why doesn't she smack him?"

"Smack little child?" Cooracardie sounded disgusted. "My people *good* people . . . no punish little children. Never."

Tabalu had begun to join the fun in his own way. Chasing around the fire with two dogs at his heels, he made the animals bark and leap at the Kukatja guests.

The game was going too far, even for the patient head-man. He got up and called after the boy. But Tabalu paid no attention. At last the headman gave chase. The distance between them shortened; Tabalu ran fast, but the headman's legs were a good deal longer.

Tabalu decided to break for cover. Streaking away from the fire, he made straight for Cooracardie's shelter. For a moment, it looked as if the headman was giving up the pursuit. Then, suddenly, Tabalu gave a squeak of pleasure. He had found his brother and his friends.

The headman, listening to the small boy's excited chatter, turned back. A moment later he was blocking the doorway, and the shelter went dark.

Cooracardie, looking unhappy and subdued, was obviously obeying the headman's orders. He went to fetch flaring torches from the fire and then fixed them inside the shelter in cracks between the stones. The chores completed, he sat down on the floor between Peter and the headman.

Loritja spoke.

"Loritja say . . ." Cooracardie fumbled, "I say what he say to you."

Again Loritja spoke in the strange, flowing language.

"Loritja angry you come here. More angry I take you here."

"Tell him it wasn't your fault," said Anita. "We first came on our own."

The headman nodded.

"Loritja ask why you spy."

"We wanted to know why we weren't allowed to stay in the camp. And we wanted to see what was happening."

"You afraid?" translated Cooracardie.

"A bit."

"Headman say you make me give you secrets of my people."

"I suppose we did," admitted Peter.

Cooracardie shook his head. "I tell Loritja *I* give secrets. *You* no bad. *I* do bad thing."

"That's not true," objected Anita. "We asked a lot of questions. And you *knew* we'd go snooping around the camp on our own, if you didn't take us. Tell Loritja you were sort of keeping an eye on us. What else could you have done? We gave you no choice."

Loritja smiled, and suddenly the stern face was full of good humor and gentleness. "Cooracardie could have told me," he said in good English. "He should not have concealed from me your night visits."

Cooracardie gaped at the headman. "I no know . . ."

"No, you didn't know I can speak English, boy. Do you know why I asked you to translate for me?"

"I no know."

"It was the quickest way of finding out the truth about all three of you. Cooracardie, your fair friends have seen what only the men of your own tribe have been permitted to witness in the past."

"I bad. You punish. I take punishes."

"No, boy. You're only a child."

"Please!" There were tears in Cooracardie's eyes. "I no child. I, man. I come home for becoming man, Loritja."

"You've come home too soon. You will be sent back to Hermannsburg Mission. . . . It won't be so lonely this time. Both your parents are working there now."

"My mother . . ."

"She's out of hospital, Cooracardie."

"When I come back?"

"In two years perhaps." Loritja touched Cooracardie's face. "When your English is better." He turned to Peter and Anita. "You will sleep here. I'll speak to you in the morning."

"I have a message for you, Peter," said Loritja. "Your father is recovering from the accident which has brought you here . . . thanks to the Kukatja who rescued him."

"Thank you, sir."

"When will we be going home?" asked Anita.

"You've seen too much of our ceremonies and rites. I'm afraid I can't let you go until you understand us better than you do at the moment."

Peter's suspicions returned. Perhaps the Aranda people were cannibals, perhaps they weren't; what mattered now was that he and Anita were in their hands. "We *are* prisoners," he whispered to her.

Loritja frowned. "Pay attention! I wish to speak to you of my people. . . . This is a country where people and land have been united for thousands of years. . . ."

The sun, lifting from the distant sands like a weary camel, climbed the morning. Steep rock faces emerged from their morning grayness. The colors of crags and columns rose from shell pink to flame red until they glowed as if a furnace was burning inside every stone.

"Yes," said Loritja, "take a good look at this blaze . . . this land of fire. Our sun has become a killer."

The animals, which had been wandering around the ashes of the campfire, were in retreat. Shaab, picking up his gawky legs, was making for the sparse shade of the ghost gums. The dingo had slunk inside a shelter. A little wallaby, which was mothering small animals of the guinea-pig family, was nudging her horde behind a broken wall. Even Tabalu's parakeet was making off in the direction of the canyon. Only Cooracardie's lizard stayed put, lying across the entrance of the shelter in the full heat of day.

"The sun has become a killer," repeated Loritja. "Once there was rain. And the rain fed the rivers, and the rivers fed the soil. And from the soil grew green grasses which fed kangaroo in great numbers. My people wandered through the land, and the kangaroo and the grasses fed them well." Loritja's voice had assumed the alien tones of the aboriginal chant. "Then came the white man. He brought his cattle and his sheep, and his animals fed off our lands. Some of us went to work for the white man, and he became a part of our life. But *his* life was different from ours. He was not a wanderer. He built a permanent home and filled it with objects. He brought clothes and tea, machines . . . and alcohol. Many of our young began to want these things. They left us. They gave up the wandering and the hunting and they deserted the spirit world of the past, which had always been our home and our strength.

"The aboriginals have become aliens in their own country. The civilization of the machines has not accepted them— neither the young, who deserted their ancestral ways, nor us who have remained faithful to the ancient wisdoms.

"What of those of my people who have remained wanderers of the bush? The old, who have knowledge of this our life, have been dying away, and there are not enough young to follow in their steps. Many old aboriginals like myself fear that our race will neither continue in existence as it is, nor be allowed to become a part of the modern age. Yes . . . we're in danger of dying out."

"There's Cooracardie," said Anita, quietly.

"Yes, there are a few who live the traditions of their

people . . . a few who are loyal."

"Then why are you sending Cooracardie away?"

"Because we surely will die as a people unless we learn what *your* people know. We and you share this land. We shall have to fight for it together or perish. . . . If we don't fight the killer sun together we shall die together."

"But what can you do about the sun?"

"Your people, Peter, have a new knowledge called science. How are we to be saved if not by the new knowledge? For more than *ten* years this land has not seen rain. The rivers are dry. The pastures have been swallowed by the sand. Millions of animals have died—your cattle and our kangaroo. The dying is going on now, today. Two hundred and fifty thousand square miles of good land have turned into desert—red sand, rock, dead trees. The land is dying."

"How can anyone stop it?"

"The government could bring us water. . . . Oh, I know it would cost much money. But even that wouldn't be enough. To save ourselves and the country, we shall have to understand one another. Your people have much knowledge of one kind, mine have knowledge of another kind. All of it will be needed if this land is to live . . . all of it."

Cooracardie and Tabalu had crept into the shelter, and squatted down beside the headman.

"This boy," Loritja looked at Cooracardie, "has revealed to you secrets of our people. Yet—what is more—he has revealed to me the future. Cooracardie *is* the future. He has saved you two from the killer sun, and he is willing to share with you the wisdom of his own people. He has recognized, young as he is, that our only enemy is the sun—your enemy and ours."

Peter stared at Loritja's serene face. "Then you don't mind about Cooracardie telling us. . . ."

"Cooracardie is a child. Therefore he hasn't been able to tell you *enough*."

They sat on through the burning hours while Loritja talked of his people's customs and beliefs.

He talked of *altjira*, dreamtime, as a period of recollecting the wisdom of the ancestors, as a time of contemplation during which deep thought extracted knowledge from the mind of the dreamer. It was a unique knowledge that revealed to the aboriginal how to survive in deserts that killed men and beasts despite modern machines, knowledge that taught him to read the minutest signs of earth, sun, and moon.

Loritja talked of the aboriginal heroes of thousands of years ago and of the songs and dances that celebrated their deeds and kept alive their teachings.

When the headman fell silent, Peter and Anita hardly noticed that he was leaving them. Even after he had gone out of their shelter, it was as if the changing desert itself was continuing to speak. The rocks were turning purple and lilac until the colors faded, leaving an unearthly landscape of burned-out stone and dying earth.

"It must be harder for *them*," said Peter.

"Maybe not." Anita stroked the lizard Cooracardie. "I think he was telling us that it's no easier for us to understand *them*, than it is for them to understand us."

"Seems nothing is easy when different kinds of people have to work together. And if people *don't* pull together, they lay themselves wide open to the *real* killers. I've been thinking, Anita. . . . In some places the destroyers are typhoons, or floods, disease, or dictators who make war. Here, it's the sun."

"You have listened wisely." Loritja stood in the entrance, a flaming torch held aloft. "You will be welcome *inside* our camp if ever you return to us."

Anita jumped to her feet. "We can go home . . . ? Now?"

"Yes, you can go. Cooracardie and Tabalu will accompany you as far as Hermannsburg." Loritja picked up the chattering Tabalu. "Cooracardie, *you* had better explain to him. He'll have to leave his camel here. Shaab wouldn't be able to keep up with the station wagon Anita's father is driving . . . and Shaab is a little too big to travel inside. But I expect Mr. Landson will allow your young brother to take the dingo and his parakeet. Come, take your lizard. . . . You two haven't collected any *more* familiars, have you?"

Morning

THE SUN, LIFTING FROM THE DISTANT SANDS like a weary camel, climbed the morning. Steep rock faces emerged from their dawn grayness. The colors of crags and columns rose from shell pink to flame red until they glowed as if a furnace was burning inside every stone.

"Rock," said Bill Ellwood. "Rock, sand, dead trees. . . . Two hundred and fifty thousand square miles of land gone to waste. You know, Mac, now you've told me about Cooracardie and his people, I can see why Peter acted funny when I talked about opening up new mines here. . . . He's right. What's needed is water for growing trees and grass."

"There's room for mines as well as for growing things," I said. "In any case you couldn't have your mines in the middle of a desert. You too would need water."

"I guess some of the money Australia's going to earn from the mine at Mount Tom Price could pay for getting water a long way inland."

"A long enough way, Peter thinks, to save the homelands, of the aboriginals. . . . Have you noticed? They've stopped beating their drums."

Bill nodded. "Maybe they've found the truck."

"Or what's left of it," I said. "This trip's been dis-appointing for you."

"No, I wouldn't say so. I found what I was looking for . . . the people, not the opal cave that belongs to them. And their kinda country of course. It's a strange thing," said Bill, staring into the dead ashes of the fire, now a little heap of white glossamer dust, "the way the bush nearly killed us—both Peter and me. . . ."

Yes, this country had almost killed them, but in the end it had made them what they are—Peter, a geologist special-ized in the construction of waterways—Bill, a miner. The one had discovered his aim in life through the friendship of an ancient people, the other through the burned-out fires of a thousands-of-years-old stone.

I could have told Ellwood that I too had been made into what I am by this land. If I'd stayed at home, in England,

I'd now be flying jet airliners from one crowded city to another. I'd be flying at thirty thousand feet, in a no man's land of cloud with not a rock or a tree in sight. Instead I have it both ways; I can go up into the sky or I can fly so low in my little plane that I can see the flame-red rocks and the rose-colored sands and the campfires of the only people who ever mastered the bush.

I couldn't survive in this desert as the aboriginals do; yet, flying low above them, I feel that I too belong here. And I'm glad I do because here is a piece of world as unspoiled as it was on the morning the universe came alive. Yet it's big enough for the future—for mines, for farming, for *any* man who cares for it and who isn't out to make his living the easy way.

"You've told me nothing about yourself," said Bill. "About the air search for Peter's father . . . *your* end of it.

"That was nothing . . . just part of my job."

"What a job! Trying to locate a car in this wilderness."

"Reckon it is. Mr. Landson was one of the lucky fellows. The aboriginals found him in time."

The camels had gone. Cooracardie and Tabalu had gone. And the truck stood parked in the shade of the rocks.

"You keep hearing of people who get bushed," said the driver, "but you never think it could happen to you."

"It wasn't your fault, Roger," said Peter.

"I should have known better. . . ." He turned to Ellwood. "At this time of year we get cyclones around the northwest coast. And during these gales you get more willy-willies inland. The willies change the patches of bull dust, so you get the loose dust where there'd been none before. . . . I didn't think enough about it. . . . Turned the truck over on her side. Broke my arm. . . . Couldn't dig myself out. . . ."

"We'll get you to a doctor inside of three days," Peter told him.

"I'm not complaining," said Roger. "Your aboriginal lads made a good job of splinting the arm."

"The aboriginals?" asked Bill.

"Cooracardie." Peter smiled. "If he weren't so busy in the Health Service—working among his people in the bush—he'd be a doctor by now. . . . Well, Cooracardie and Tabalu are on their way home. We'll be going on by ourselves. The truck's all right. I think we should start about six."

"Better get some sleep," I suggested. Searching for the truck, and then digging it out in this punishing heat, must have been exhausting. Peter looked extremely tired.

"Yes, I'll have a rest. But let's have some tea first." He went and picked up the kettle which was still standing beside last night's burned-out fire.

Bill Ellwood took it out of his hand. "Let me do this, Peter. . . . I'd like to."

MADELAINE DUKE is the kind of person one normally expects to meet only in fiction. Physician, scientist and at the end of the war an officer of British Intelligence, she is also a best-selling author. Dr. Duke has traveled all over the world, and THE SECRET PEOPLE is a result of time actually spent in the bush country of Australia.

She holds a B.Sc. from St. Andrews University and an M.B. and Ch.B. in medicine from Edinburgh University. Dr. Duke is married to a physician and lives in a seventeenth-century home in Sussex, England.

KEN LONGTEMPS was educated in New Haven and received a B.S.A. in Illustration from the Rhode Island School of Design. He has done a considerable amount of books, both jackets and illustrations, and has worked with most of the major publishers in New York. Mr. Longtemps is a resident of Brooklyn, New York.